Back
to
Black

Kyoko M.

A Novella from The Black Parade
series

The Black Parade
The Deadly Seven: Stories from The Black Parade
series
She Who Fights Monsters
Back to Black
The Holy Dark

Other Works by Kyoko M
Of Cinder and Bone

Cover art by Marginean Anca

Edited by Andi Marlowe

Gaze no more in the bitter glass
The demons, with their subtle guile,
Lift up before us when they pass,
Or only gaze a little while;
For there a fatal image grows,
With broken boughs, and blackened leaves,
And roots half hidden under snows
Driven by a storm that ever grieves.
For all things turn to barrenness
In the dim glass of outer weariness,
Made when God slept in times of old.
-The Two Trees, W.B. Yeats

CHAPTER ONE

Dying's a bitch, and I would know.

To be fair, I didn't actually remember what happened when I died. It was over a year ago, and the soul is a radically different entity from the mind. In case you're wondering, yes, there is an afterlife, and no, I can't tell you what it looks like. Sorry. Life is full of disappointments.

How then, Ms. Jordan Amador, you ask, can you say dying is a bitch if you don't remember your own death? Well, I remember everything up until my death, and that was certainly a bitch. The archdemon Belial had kidnapped me with the intent of sacrificing me so that he could open a portal into the body of the archangel Michael, therefore allowing him unlimited power and access to influencing the innocent people of the world to do his bidding. Long story short, we stopped him, but I died in the process, and in excruciating pain, I might add.

Much like right now.

Ever had one of those out-of-body experiences? Not the kind that you'd see in the movie *Ghost*, but a true case of an otherworldly viewing of your own self. Detachment. Like someone plucked away the strings that connected you to yourself, and the byproduct was that you almost felt like the consequences of the world didn't directly affect you.

That was me.

I was hanging from two thick, nasty braided ropes: one at each of my wrists, cutting off circulation. A spotlight illuminated my body and its myriad of problems: broken ribs, fractured eye-socket, busted lip, cracked teeth, and what felt like severe internal bleeding. It hurt to breathe. It hurt to exist, really.

My current predicament came at the hands of a short brunette with matted curly hair, a pug nose, and pale skin courtesy of her father, Lamont Brooks. Mr. Brooks was a loan shark from Detroit who had swindled my estranged father and then tried to kill him. I took issue with that. My pseudo-brother, the archangel Gabriel — long story — and I busted Lamont and his whole operation several months ago, and sent her old man up the river.

And she took issue with that.

In my defense, these clowns got lucky. It was late at night, I was exhausted, alone, and under-prepared for six hulking guys in masks jumping me in the parking lot, beating me senseless, and dragging me into a van. I had no idea where we were, but I knew that no one was going to save me if I didn't save myself.

I'd tried. The ropes were too tight and I had no use of my hands. Brooks' daughter, Bridgett as I overheard one of the mooks call her, worked me over for hours, and I had no energy left. Figures. I'd saved the world twice now and yet I was going to be delivered to fate by some snot-nosed bitch with Daddy issues. Life had a cruel sense of humor.

She wanted to break me, and in some ways, she had. I couldn't pretend like there was a one-liner to get me out of this hellhole. No backup. No literal Deus Ex Machina. I had lost everyone in my life — my husband, my best friend, my adoptive brother, even my deadbeat dad, and my mother long before any of them — and now I would lose my life.

The deranged, laughably short daughter of a Detroit mobster stepped back into the spotlight surrounding me, and I could barely see her through my working eye. She looked smug. Joke's on her. Amador women always go out the way God intended.

"Any last words?"

I summoned one last reedy breath and smiled at her through my ruined mouth.

"Your daddy hit like a little bitch."

Snarling, Bridgett lifted the tire iron and swung it at my head.

Before it could land, a long, terrifying wolf's howl echoed through the room.

Bridgett stopped dead and whirled around. I heard the rustle of clothing as if her hired goons had done the same. "What the hell was that?"

"I dunno," one Einstein replied.

"Go check it out, asshole. I'm not paying you to stand there!" she hissed, her back to me. I thought about spitting another gob of blood into her hair, but I didn't have enough saliva. Bummer.

I couldn't see through the veil of darkness thanks to the stupid spotlight, but I could still hear relatively well. Footsteps on concrete. Muttered curses as the goons filtered outside to see what had made that eerie noise. I couldn't keep my eye open anymore and let it drop closed. The pain had given way to blessed numbness not long ago, but it wasn't a good thing. The creeping blackness tugging at my mind wasn't sleep, but death. It curled a long forefinger at me, promising an escape from the wretched state of my life.

In death, I would see my beloved archangel one more time.

Maybe, just maybe, it wasn't such a bad idea.

A man's scream ripped through the night.

I jerked awake, fresh adrenaline pumping through my weary veins, forcing my working eye open again. Gunshots, but not concentrated ones. Panic fire. Something growled in the distance and then I heard doors slamming as some of the men ran back inside.

"What is it?" Bridgett demanded, and the anger had given way to panic as well. Serves her right, the little cunt.

"S-Some kind of, I don't know, rabid dog!" one of her men sputtered, metal clicking as he reloaded a magazine in his gun. "It's out there tearing them to shreds!"

"Then shoot it, you moron!"

"No, you don't get it. The bullets didn't work. It just…shrugged them off or something. I don't know what the hell it is, but it can't get through the door. If we just stay in here, we'll—"

Another gunshot, but not from a pistol. Louder, as if it had come from a rifle. The man who had been speaking hit the concrete, dead as a doornail.

Crack!

Another man hit the deck, and then I heard sneakers on the concrete as the other four fled towards the outside, deciding to face whatever terror lay out there rather than be shot in the head. Screams greeted them. A thick, tearing sound, like fangs through flesh. Then eerie silence.

Bridgett screamed and fired into the rafters blindly, until her gun clicked empty.

She threw the gun to the floor and bellowed, "What do you want?"

Her frenzied pants were all I could hear.

Then a woman's voice—hard as a diamond—spoke from the shadows.

"Die confused."

Crack!

Bridgette tumbled to the floor, her doll eyes open, a perfect round exit wound through her wide forehead.

My last breath came out a vindictive wheeze.

"*Vaya con dios*, bitch."

I had never been in a hedge maze before.

Sure, I had seen them on TV, but I'd never had the chance to visit one. Before my life went to shit, I'd lived in Albany, New York working as a waitress by day, Seer by night, and though my married life had been quite lovely, the opportunity never presented itself to go inside a hedge maze.

And yet, here I stood, surrounded by eight-foot-high, neatly trimmed greenery with occasional crimson roses poking out, and flat grass beneath my black Reeboks. It wasn't bright out, though. I examined the darkening sky and realized it was probably sunset. All this green would turn navy with the shadows in no time at all. I had to get out of here soon, and yet didn't know why I knew that.

"You know exactly why, my pet."

I froze. Oh no. Not him.

I swallowed hard and forced my rigid body to turn around.

The archdemon Belial stood four feet away, smiling sweetly, a red rose clutched in his hand.

Shit.

If one didn't know him, Belial would actually be a feast for the eyes. He regularly changed his appearance based on whatever he needed to do on earth, but being a Prince of Hell had its own habits. White privilege practically dripped off of his personality, and so his appearance followed suit: alabaster skin, long, jet-black hair, icy blue eyes, a narrow nose, elegantly thin but sensual lips, and an almost insultingly luscious, hard, contoured body. Said luscious body was currently encased in all-black attire: a dress shirt, slacks, and shoes, except for his tie, which was a shimmering blue-silver hue. The only thing that offset it were his wings—enormous things that arched up over either side of his shoulders and swept against the back of his knees. Each feather was pitch-black and glowed orange-red at the edges as if it were on fire, as a sign of his fall from grace. He wasn't unusually tall—perhaps right at six feet—but the way he held himself, like a tiger whose domain knew no limits—always made him seem bigger than he actually was.

Then again, it wasn't like I was some looming giant. I was average height and sleight of frame. People tended to underestimate me since I wasn't strikingly beautiful or really memorable-looking in general: dark shoulder-length hair, brown eyes, *morena* skin. While I was agile, I could only hit so hard. He knew that, and constantly delighted in it every time we interacted.

Belial brought the rose up to his nose and took a sniff, sighing. "Beautiful, isn't it?"

I balled my hands into fists and aimed a glare at him. "So I'm dead, then? This is Hell? Why else would you be standing in front of me since I stabbed you in the heart the last time we were together?"

Belial clucked his tongue. "So melodramatic, Jordan, dear. You're not dead, but you are..."

He licked those pretty lips of his. "...in rather bad shape, I'll say. Your defenses lie in tatters around you. That's how I am here."

I eyed him. "So...this is a dream?"

He nodded once. A long breath escaped me. "Oh. Well, that's nice. I'm going to wake up now, so fuck off."

I shut my eyes and concentrated. I wasn't great at lucid dreaming, but in the past, it always worked if I chanted 'wake up' in rapid succession with utter commitment to it. Silence. Nothing happened. I was still in the middle of a maze with my mortal enemy. Great.

"I'm afraid it won't be quite that easy," the demon said patiently. "You almost died, from what I can tell. You're stuck here until your spiritual energy is restored."

I crossed my arms. "And you just conveniently showed up, huh?"

He smiled. "I thought you might miss me."

"Yes," I deadpanned. "I always miss people who murder me and completely rip my life apart. Get out of my head or I'll make you."

"Oh, it's not quite that simple, my pet," he said, casually strolling towards me, spinning the red rose between his long fingers. I tensed, staying put, but ready to fight at a moment's notice. "It's not just your head. This is a shared space. You are a talented Seer, but you don't know everything. Tell me what you remember about dreams."

"Why should I?"

"Humor me."

I took a deep breath and restrained myself from punching him. "Dreams allow long distance contact between Seers, angels, and demons. It's like a form of telepathy between the spiritual community, but it requires dedication and concentration. Obviously, I have neither since you wormed your way in here."

"That's rudimentary, but correct. However, you're missing some details. You've been to the void where souls pass through to Judgment, and that is its own separate plane of existence. Dreams exist in a similar state. All those anointed or damned connect to this space whether we realize it or not during slumber. If one has the wherewithal, they can find a person of interest at any time when they are asleep and unguarded."

He held the rose out to me, his smile suddenly quite sharp. "Hence our reunion."

I took the rose, snapped the stem in half, and threw it away. "Get to the point, asshole. What do you want?"

Belial breathed in, as if summoning more of his patience, and fixed me with a steady stare. The five archdemons of Hell had the same mark of royalty—

slitted pupils instead of round ones. He reminded me of a snake when he stared at me like that, and it wasn't far from the truth. There was nothing he wanted more than to devour me whole. I suppressed a small shudder at the thought.

"To chase you."

I stared at him. "What?"

He grinned. "You heard me, Seer. Run."

"What are you, nine? I'm not playing Hide-and-Seek with you, especially since you just said I'm mostly dead right now."

"It's less of Hide-and-Go-Seek," he said, folding his arms behind him. "More Hide-and-Go-Freak, if that is still the colloquialism."

It took me several seconds to speak, and the response came through my clenched teeth. "You have exactly three seconds to get away from me before I strangle you to death."

"Skipping the foreplay, are we?"

"Look, if you're going to try to kill me or assault me, we're going to square off. I'm not a coward. I don't run. I've killed you before and I'll do it again, with or without my body."

He arched a thin eyebrow. "You will, will you? Go ahead. Summon a weapon. Kill me, Seer. I dare you."

I lowered my right hand and focused all my energy into forming a Smith & Wesson .9mm semiautomatic. It materialized in my hand—heavy, formidable, and reliable.

I raised the gun to his head and pulled the trigger.

Belial lifted his hand and *caught the fucking bullet*.

I stared at the barrel of the gun in disbelief and then emptied the clip.

I couldn't follow the motion, but I knew that I'd seen his arm and shoulder move. He opened his hand and all of the slugs clinked together on his palm.

Well, shit.

Belial tipped his hand over and let the bullets hit the grass. He looked up at me again and the serpentine smile on his lips made me shiver.

"Run."

I threw the gun at him.

It whacked him dead in the forehead and he snarled in pained surprise. That was my only victory before I turned and ran at a dead sprint into the maze.

Right. Left. Right. Left. Left, left, left, right, right, left, right.

I didn't think about it. No time to think. Act. Flee. Survive.

I'd been running for what felt like eons before my weary body forced me to stop. I found a corner and knelt in the cold, dark leaves of one of the maze shrubs, panting for air. This didn't make any sense. Why had he brought me here? What was the point? And how was I going to get out of here?

I strained to listen for footsteps, but knew there wouldn't be any. Belial was a hunter. He'd had my scent in his nose ever since he stumbled across me over a year ago. Once upon a time, I'd been confused about why he became so obsessed with me, until I discovered that he'd had a servant named Zora — a

Seer, like me — who also shared her soul with the angel Uriel. She'd been his informer until they were caught and Heaven banished her to Purgatory, leaving both Belial and Uriel half of a whole until Judgment Day. In any other case, that sounded like a Shakespearean tragedy, but it wasn't. He wanted me to take her place, to spend eternity kneeling at his feet, licking his boots and whatever else he wanted to put in front of me.

I suppressed yet another shudder and thought hard about what I'd been taught by the angels. There had to be a way to get out of this nightmare. Some kind of trick.

I ran through what Belial had told me so far. Energy. My spiritual reserves were at zero. How could I replenish them? Sleep was usually the easiest option, but clearly that wouldn't be fast enough. Sooner or later, he'd find me.

I flinched as the rose bush dug into my arm, batting it away. My skin tingled where a thorn had pricked me. I glanced down to see that I wasn't actually bleeding, but there was a phantom sensation over my brown skin. Something familiar.

I checked the corner of the maze again and plucked one of the roses, smelling it. Coolness breathed through me. Comforting. Almost like when the archangel Gabriel had healed me before.

"Son of a bitch," I muttered, plucking one of the rose petals. The base of the petal had some kind of soft white glow to it, like dewdrops in sunlight. I let it sit in my palm and felt it absorb into my skin, travel down my arm, and settle in the center of my chest.

I snatched rose after rose from the bush and plucked their petals, eventually creating a bed of them beneath my knees. I flattened my hands over them and concentrated, absorbing it all into me as fast as I could.

"Well," Belial said dryly from directly behind me. "It took you long enough."

I didn't offer another scathing remark. Instead, I whipped my right leg around at his head as hard as I possibly could.

Belial brought up his forearm and blocked it. I didn't want him to grab my leg, so I curled my leg in and landed in a crouch. I pounced up towards his smirking face, launching into a flurry of jabs and straight shots. My fists breezed past his cheeks by mere millimeters, so close that I felt the flutter of his black hair over my knuckles. I tried to knee him in the groin, but he blocked it. Truth be told, I knew he was toying with me, but I wouldn't give him the satisfaction of surrendering. I'd go out fighting. After all, I had before.

"You've gotten better since we last fought," the archdemon mused, twisting to one side as I aimed a kick at his knee. "Faster, more confident. To a less able demon, you'd actually present a threat."

He was lecturing me in the middle of a fight. Pure fury filled me. My limbs felt like bars of white-hot lead. I swung harder and swifter, fueled by the need to make the bastard bleed. He slapped my arms aside and smoothly dodged everything else without even the slightest effort. Screw it. If I was going out, I'd take him with me.

I stepped back and concentrated what little energy I'd been able to absorb into something huge, metal, and unmistakably deadly. My right shoulder ached from the weight as it materialized in both hands.

I'd summoned an RPG.

Belial's eyes went wide, and then narrowed to slits. "You wouldn't dare."

I smiled. "Watch me."

Just as I pulled the trigger, Belial grabbed the barrel and tipped it straight up. The rocket sparked out of the barrel and exploded several hundred feet up in the cool, dark night sky like a lone, neglected firework.

I fell on my ass in the grass and the launcher flopped right behind me out of reach. I tried to scramble to my feet, but by then, it was too late. Belial slammed me down onto the grass and pinned my wrists, straddling my waist so I couldn't shove myself back up. My heart thudded against my chest, in my throat as I struggled in vain. Not enough energy. I was caught. Prey.

"You know," he said slowly, his snake eyes roving over my face and neck. "I almost forgot how cute it is when you try to resist me. I know you won't believe me, but I have missed you, pet. I missed that fire. No one else on earth has your kind of fire."

"Save it," I spat. "I don't care how powerful you are; you're not getting into my pants. I'll die first."

Something predatory skittered through those pale eyes. "Is that so? Why do I seem to recall a very different reaction to my advances in recent history?"

Hot blood rushed up through my cheeks. I tried not to conjure up images, but they crashed against the surface of my mind anyway. A hotel in the middle of Bumfuck Nowhere, Georgia. Cheap bed, ugly sheets, ratty carpet. I'd punched him over and over, screaming how much I hated him, seconds before he rolled us over on the bed and kissed me senseless. I wanted to forget that moment, erase it, delete it, but it wouldn't happen no matter how hard I tried.

"Doesn't matter," I growled. "It won't happen again."

"I think you know better," the demon whispered. He stretched my arms out above my head, nestling them in the rose petals, and leaned over my neck. His lips brushed the side of my throat, lightly, over my pulse, so delicate it could have been a gentle breeze.

"Admit it, Seer. Some part of you has missed me."

"The part that wants to kill you, maybe."

He chuckled, and hearing that deep, velvet voice from so close sent a buzzing sensation rushing down the front of my body, awakening parts of me that it shouldn't have. "That is the part I have missed most of all. Why else do we keep finding ourselves in this same position, playing this same game over and over?"

He lifted up enough to brush those plush lips against the shell of my ear. "How long can you resist me, Jordan?"

I met his gaze as he rose over me. "Forever, demon."

~ 17 ~

Belial tilted his head until his lips hovered over mine, his silken hair sweeping over my cheeks, his long lashes brushing mine.

"Nothing lasts forever, my pet."

I woke up screaming.

CHAPTER TWO

It sounds obvious as hell, but getting beaten to death *hurt*.

I crashed into consciousness, and my body proceeded to give me a detailed report of everything that was FUBAR. My swollen face throbbed with every heartbeat. My ribs felt like they'd been splintered like uncooked spaghetti noodles and then unceremoniously shoved into my lungs. The muscles in my stomach were wound tight in knots, most likely from whatever internal damage Bridgett had done. Thankfully, the little bitch hadn't bothered with my legs, so they were relatively fine except for the dull ache of pure exhaustion.

Every breath was agony. I couldn't get enough air. My lungs wouldn't expand due to the tightness of the bandages around my upper torso. Tears welled up and spilled out of my eyes as I tried to move, but none of my nerve endings got the message. The pain gave way to pure panic. I couldn't move. I was paralyzed. God help me, *I was paralyzed*.

Then a woman's voice spoke in the darkness again.

"If you don't stop that wheezing, you'll pass out again."

My eyes darted back and forth, eventually adjusting to the dark. I was in a hotel room and a cheap one by the way the springs of the bed underneath me dug into my spine. The silvery moonlight spilled in from a dingy window to my right, illuminating the long, jean-clad legs of a woman. A bright orange spot glowed for a second and dimmed. I smelled cigarette smoke a moment later as she exhaled.

"Focus. Breathe slowly. One of your lungs collapsed earlier and I had to heal it, so I need to know if you've recovered yet."

"W-Who…?"

"No questions," the woman said. "Breathe."

Frustration bubbled up through my raw body. "W-Who…are…you?"

"Shut up and do as I say or I'll leave your ass here to die."

I gritted my teeth, wanting to defy her on principle alone, but I didn't have a choice. I focused all my energy on getting my lungs to fill with air. More tears eased down the side of my face as the sharp pain lanced through my chest, but after about the eighth time I did it, I could feel the oxygen expanding into normal breaths.

"Good," the woman said. "Guess I'm better at this than I thought."

"You're…a…Seer?"

"Congrats," she said, finally standing up. "You've stated the obvious. Rest. I've got more work to do. You can interrogate me when you're not half-dead."

I had just enough energy to imitate Billy Crystal. "Only…*mostly*…dead."

The woman exhaled through her nose. It sounded like a snort hiding a laugh. Go me. "I'm definitely going to regret saving someone who quotes the fucking *Princess Bride* to their savior. Get some rest. We'll talk soon."

She still hadn't stepped all the way into the moonlight, so I passed out with only an image of a lit cigarette in my mind, floating brightly in the void.

I didn't dream. Thank God.

When I woke the second time, the pain had lessened. The swelling around my eyes was minor, only puffy as if I'd had a bad reaction to something. Breathing still hurt like a bitch, but instead of feeling like I had a porcupine inside me, it was that irritating prick similar to getting a cramp after a long run. I couldn't feel my face well enough to know if my nose was still broken, but it didn't feel terrible either, so maybe she'd fixed it. Truth be told, I really wasn't looking forward to seeing my reflection. I probably looked like Quasimodo.

The room was empty this time. Judging by the faint sunlight, I guessed it was morning. I checked my watch to confirm it and nearly paled as I realized the date. I'd been unconscious for *two whole days*. Merciful God.

In small, painful movements, I managed to push myself into a sitting position. The room had two twin beds, and the other one was rumpled all to hell. One dresser, what appeared to be a tiny bathroom across from it, and an equally tiny closet beside it. The door was straight ahead. No sign of my mysterious Good Samaritan Seer friend. Weird.

Standing took nearly everything out of me. My hands trembled as I clutched the dresser to stay upright. The room swirled and pirouetted, eventually stabilizing after I held still for a long moment. I shuffled one foot at a time to the door and opened it.

A fucking hellhound stood on the other side of the door.

Like every hellhound I'd ever laid eyes on, he was every bit of three feet tall and covered in shaggy black fur that still smelled faintly of sulfur. Creatures of Hell weren't allowed on Earth, but hellhounds were unfortunately permitted on a technicality. The demons would take a normal dog and pour copious amounts of demonic energy into it until the dog turned into a ravenous monster that could reduce a stadium full of people into Spaghetti-O's in a matter of minutes. They could be killed, but certainly not by a mostly dead Seer who could barely hold herself up. I was thoroughly screwed.

The hellhound locked its red eyes on me and bared its enormous yellow fangs. I don't know if you've ever stood in front of a growling dog before, but it is *not* a pleasant experience. Take that pants-shitting sound and multiply it by infinity and you'll finally have a glimpse of what I just described. Primal fear exploded out of me all at once as the hound hunched down in attack position, ready to pounce and rip my throat out.

"Oy!"

I jumped as I heard the woman's voice again, only this time she stood on the sidewalk with two plastic paper cups and a plain white paper bag.

She was about two inches taller than me and even darker-skinned than I was. Her black hair was short enough to just barely touch her chin and the front swoop was mostly white, like Rogue from the X-

Men. She looked to be mid-forties, but her body didn't show it at all; her frame consisted of voluptuous curves piled on top of pure, sculpted muscle. She had high, pronounced cheekbones and striking russet eyes narrowed at the hellbeast in front of me.

"Run!" I said, glancing side to side in the room in hopes of finding a weapon. "I'll distract it so you can—"

"Ace, heel!" the woman snapped at the hound, walking closer. "No one's in the mood for your bullshit right now, you dumb mutt."

The hellhound glanced at her and then sat down on its haunches, its growl dying down to a low murmur.

My jaw promptly unhinged from my face and hit the floor.

"That's better," the woman said, and then glanced at me as if I were an idiot. "Wouldja go back in the room before someone sees you? Do you want breakfast or not?"

She pushed past me and shut the door with her foot. I turned around, my trembling arm still pointing at the door.

"But...how..."

"Long story, kid," she said, setting the coffee and food on the dresser. "I'll fill you in later. We need to eat and then get on the road before someone finds us."

"Okay," I said finally, holding out both hands. "What do you mean 'we'? You still haven't told me who you are, why you helped me, where we are, or where we're going."

She rolled her eyes. "God, you are mouthy. Wish Gabriel would've warned me."

A cold shock spread through me. "Gabriel? As in the archangel Gabriel?"

"The very same," she said, tearing open a sugar packet and dumping it into one of the paper cups. "What a babe. Too bad they're all basically really pretty Ken dolls, or I'd have hit that from here to Los Angeles."

In spite of the shock, a blush curled over my cheeks. "Can you, uh, not talk about him like that? He's kind of like my older brother. Or he was, at least."

She eyed me, sipping the coffee. "I got that vibe from him. He was very tight-lipped when I asked him about you, but I could tell you were friends."

"Look, I'm grateful that you saved me, but please, would you just answer my damn questions already? Otherwise, I'll take my chances with Darth Scooby Doo out there."

"Fine," she groused, picking a chocolate iced donut out of the bag. "Name's Myra Bennett. You already know that I'm a Seer like you, but I've only been a Seer for a couple months."

"Where did you come from, Mrs. Bennett?"

She arched an eyebrow and I pointed to her wedding band. She grunted in affirmation. "I live in Houston. Ex-military. My Awakening happened and that's how I met Gabriel. Took me a while to accept what he told me, and to tell you the truth, I wasn't all that interested. Don't care about Heaven and Hell. Nothing to do with me and mine, or so I thought."

I made my way back to the bed and she handed me a coffee. I was so damned tired that I just slurped it black. She handed me a blueberry donut to munch on as she continued. "Unfortunately, the other side didn't want to hear that. I had a visit from a demon one night and he wants to recruit me. Says if I don't do his bidding, he'll wipe out my entire family."

I shut my eyes for a second. "Shit. I'm sorry."

"Don't be. You're going to help me kill him."

I went rigid. "Excuse me?"

"Remember the part where I saved your life? You owe me one."

I stared at her. "Are…are you *blackmailing* me?"

"Nonsense," Myra said. "Blackmail implies that I have something on you. I'm guilt-tripping you."

"Gee, thanks for clearing that up," I snapped. "Where are we?"

"Calm your tits. We're still in New York, so if you need to grab some supplies from your apartment before we head out of town, we can swing past."

My God, the ovaries on this woman. I rubbed my forehead and tried to quell my temper. "How did you find me in that warehouse?"

"I've been watching you for weeks."

I spat out my coffee. "*What?*"

Myra arched an eyebrow again. "You were on the news. Wanted for murder and aiding the escape of a serial killer. I wasn't about to march right up and introduce myself if you're as crazy and dangerous as they made you out to be. Needed to see what kind of person you are and if you might be able to help me.

Your reputation is dubious at best and sinister at worst. I had to find out for myself."

"Why me? There are other Seers in the States."

She shook her head. "There are only two of them, and they're even greener than I am. I need a professional."

"Why didn't you ask Gabriel for help?"

She snorted again. "Your adoptive brother would probably object to my intentions."

I narrowed my eyes at her. "Which are?"

"Kill every one of those motherfuckers."

"He wouldn't put it in those terms," I said dryly. "But the angels are at war with the demons. If we ask for assistance, they'll lend a hand if it means wiping out a demons' nest."

"How does that old saying go? If you want something done right, do it yourself. I don't trust anything I can't see with my own two eyes. I want every one of the demons under the main one's command identified and pushing up daisies as soon as possible."

"Why not ask for protection?"

"My family's already under protection. That was the first thing Gabriel did when we met, but the angels aren't perfect. Offense is the best defense."

I raked a hand through my messy hair, thinking it over. "Look, I can appreciate that you want to keep your family safe, but this is a monumentally bad idea. Demons' nests are the deadliest places for Seers. If we're lucky, they just kill us. If we're unlucky, they'll capture us and turn us into either slaves or their personal midnight snacks."

Myra said nothing for a long stretch, sipping her coffee. "So that's it, then? All the rumors were wrong. What, did almost dying take the wind out of your sails?"

"Just what rumors have you been hearing, Mrs. Bennett?"

She smirked. "That you kicked the archdemon Mulciber's ass with nothing more than an angel feather and a go-getter attitude. That you and the archdemon Belial are fuck-buddies. That you made him fall in love with you, then murdered him in cold blood and threw his ass into the Arctic Ocean. Do I have the wrong woman, Jordan?"

"We're not fuck-buddies," I spat from between clenched teeth. "I was married."

"Oh, yeah. You popped the archangel Michael's cherry, right?"

The blush returned so furiously that I was sure my head caught on fire. I buried my burning face in my hands. "That wasn't my point. I was forced to work with Belial to defeat the Leviathan. Nothing more. I have no desire to be anywhere near that monster."

"If you say so. Still, I can't believe after all that build up, you're just a disappointment."

I lifted my head and glared. "You're not going to reverse-psychology me into helping you."

"Good point." She licked the chocolate icing off her fingers. "So how about you help me or I'll let my hellhound eat you?"

"Listen," I said rather softly. "You may have caught me at a bad time in my life, but you're out of your mind if you think for a second that I'm going to be threatened by some two-bit Seer from Houston. Think last night was me at my worst? You haven't even begun to see me at my worst. I take no joy in killing, but I will defend myself through whatever means necessary. Don't cross me, Mrs. Bennett. You might not enjoy the result."

Thick, stifling silence fell between us. She stared at me and I didn't break her gaze.

Myra's face split into an open grin. "Now that's more like it. You'll do fine. How does three thousand sound?"

I blinked. "Wait, what?"

"I'll pay you three grand to help me destroy the demons' nest in Houston."

"...you probably should have just led with that, Mrs. Bennett."

"Where's the fun in that?"

I massaged the bridge of my nose. Well, I was short on cash, my husband left me, both of my best friends weren't speaking to me, and most of the angels thought I was a traitorous harlot. Why the hell not? "I'm going to deeply regret this, but fine. I'll help you."

I extended my hand. She shook it hard and then stood up, opening the door. She paused in the archway.

"By the way? Call me Mrs. Bennett one more time and I'll break your kneecaps off and keep them in a jar by my bed."

I sighed. "I can tell this is going to be the start of something special."

She winked. "You bet your ass."

"So what's it like fucking an archangel?"

I choked on air. "Jesus *Christ*, Myra."

"What? Are you a prude?"

"I just met you like two days ago and you just asked me what it's like to have sex with my ex. Seriously? That doesn't strike you as weird?"

Myra shrugged and tapped the cigarette out the window of the white truck we were currently cruising down the highway in. We'd flown down to Texas and retrieved her truck from where she'd parked it at the airport. The hellhound, Ace, sat in the backseat with his head out the window, his huge tongue lolling out to one side, his blood-red eyes wide and disturbingly happy. Maybe he wasn't one hundred percent killing machine. There seemed to be some normal dogginess in him. "You're not with him anymore. Why should you care about sharing the gory details to a fellow sistah?"

I crossed my arms. "I don't want to talk about Michael in general, and I certainly don't want to talk about our sex life."

"That bad, huh?"

I stared out the window, hoping that my dark complexion hid the blush creeping up over my cheeks as images of said sex life sprang to mind. I'd only had one long term boyfriend before Michael, and Terrell had been serviceable in the bedroom. Not bad, got the job done, no complaints.

Michael had been—to use a terrible pun—a freaking sexpert.

It sounded unbelievable considering the man had been a virgin—angels weren't allowed to fraternize with humans any longer because it had been a big problem during the days of the Bible — but Michael had also lived as a human for a while, and I knew he had Internet access, so perhaps he'd learned a few things that way. He had taken his husbandly duties incredibly seriously. Night after night, I found myself staring up at that gorgeous face, his sea-green eyes practically glowing down at me through his brunette hair, a dangerous smirk curled over those full lips as he closed in for the kill. And don't get me started on that body — broad shoulders, a chest that would make Chris Evans get the urge to go to the gym, narrow waist, long legs, and well, he was called the Commander for a reason. He was every woman's dream.

And I'd lost him forever.

A pang of loss slid between my ribs like a knife. I buried the guilt inside me. Sulking over it would do nothing. He made his choice. So did I. We couldn't take it back.

"Drop it," I said quietly.

"Alright, don't get testy. I'll just have to wait until I get you drunk to hear about Prince Michael's boudoir antics. In the meantime, what do I need to know about you that the rumors wouldn't have told me?"

"Want the long version or the abridged version?"

Myra checked her Citizen watch. "We've got time. Long version will work."

Repeating my life story aloud made me sound like I was a few knives short of a cutlery set, but I did my best to explain how I'd completely crashed into the insane world of ghosts, angels, and demons in the worst possible way. I'd accidentally killed the man who saved my life — a careless error by a scared eighteen-year-old girl being chased by a murderous spirit — the same man who had been in love with my mother, Catalina, who had also been a Seer. I lost her at a young age and had been sent to live with her older sister, Carmensita, who saw fit to torture me at every available opportunity for nothing more than being just like my mother. Killing Andrew meant that I had two years to help one hundred souls find peace in the afterlife or my soul would go straight to Hell. Somewhere along the way, I bumped into Michael and we fell in love; a love that would have been forbidden had it not been for the Marriage of the Souls. As a Seer, technically an anointed soul, we were permitted to be married.

Until I screwed it up.

Ten months into our marriage, an angel went rogue and started killing Seers. We tried to find answers, but there were none, so we had to turn to Belial for help. We expected him to betray us, and he did, but I had been forced to ally with him over the life of a small child: Juliana Freitas. Not a day went by that I didn't think about her. I had sacrificed my life and loyalty to keep her safe, and to save the lives of a thousand innocent souls from the legendary Leviathan. We stopped it from rising and laying waste to the world, but in the process, God deemed me unworthy of staying in the company of the archangel Gabriel. Michael left not long after that, heartbroken that I'd been tempted by Belial's offer. I had tried my hardest to win him back, but he rejected me, so I packed my bags and abandoned Albany. There was nothing left for me in that city but painful memories of my former life.

And to be honest, I wasn't entirely sure there was a place for me anywhere.

"Christ," Myra sighed, tossing the spent cig out the window. "I've heard some sob stories in my time, but yours is worthy of a Lifetime movie."

"Thanks," I muttered, and took a sip from the Dasani bottle in the cup holder next to me.

"I know it probably doesn't mean much coming from a perfect stranger, but I'm sorry. You got dealt a bad hand. One of the worst I've ever heard."

I shrugged. "It's no one's fault but my own."

"Bullshit."

I glanced at her. "Sorry?"

She frowned at me. "You know how that old saying goes, 'Til death do us part?' You were married. Yeah, you screwed up on an epic scale, but you're not the only person in the relationship. He made the choice not to forgive you. He of all people should know that you were only human. You're both to blame for letting your relationship fail. Marriage isn't a walk in the park, even though everyone wants you to think it's bliss. You're supposed to fight, to lose faith, to struggle and wish you were somewhere else sometimes, but you're not supposed to actually do that. Some people go their entire lives and never find someone to love and someone who loves them equally. It's unfair and cruel, but it's life. You're an idiot for letting him walk out of yours."

"I had nothing to keep him there," I snapped. "I apologized. I said that I would atone for my sins any way he wanted me to, but he still chose to leave. What was I supposed to do? Chain myself to him?"

"Damn right. Men are thick. They think with their glands most of the time."

I shook my head and stared out the window, folding my arms over my stomach. "It's not enough to just say he's stupid. I never had what it took to be a good wife."

"Of course you did. Why do you think he left? He's still in love with you, but he didn't want to fix what the two of you broke because to him it's easier to bail. He'd rather cut out the tumor than endure the chemo."

My stomach churned. Was she right? Did he still love me? He'd been so cold the last time I saw him. He was a different person, someone I'd heard about before. Michael's soul had a sort of duality to it. His humanity made him kind, sweet, thoughtful, and compassionate. His angelic side made him stubborn, unflinching, and morally unassailable. Which part had rejected me?

"I don't want to talk about this anymore," I said finally. "Tell me how you learned how to heal me so quickly. It took me months of teaching to master it."

Myra rolled her eyes and lit a new cig. "Always been a fast learner, but Gabriel introduced me to someone he knew. He was a bit too busy to teach me more than just the rules, and so his friend Jon took over. We worked intensely over the last two months developing my powers. Anytime I wasn't at work or with my family, I practiced the craft until I felt like I had enough technique to protect them."

"What happened when the demon came for you?"

Her mouth twisted to one side, as if she were resisting a scowl. The whole of her seemed to harden into granite. She gripped the steering wheel with one hand and used the other to tug down the collar of her t-shirt.

"This."

A large, crooked scar, still held together by stitches, stared back at me from above her collarbone. I knew that kind of scar; the kind inflicted by a serrated blade. Judging from the size, it was meant to hurt, not to paralyze. A warning.

"Son of a bitch," I whispered. "I'm so sorry."

She let the cloth snap back into place over her brown skin. "I don't need sorry. I need to know if you can help me stomp them into a smear on the sidewalk."

"I won't be one hundred percent for a while, not with the damage I survived, but I can still figure out how to get rid of them."

"Where should we start?"

"Did you get a name from the asshole who gave you that scar?"

"Yeah. He told me that if I decided to 'get smart,' I should ask for Maurice."

"What's he look like?"

"Black, handsome, late thirties, six-foot-two, English accent."

"Did he tell you where to go?"

"Yeah. There's a bar downtown called The Kiln. One of his hangouts. He said I should attend the 'staff meeting' three days from now."

"No," I said. "That's a trap. He's hoping you bring in reinforcements. Odds are that if you show up, they'll kidnap you and kill anyone who helps you. I take it you've been doing surveillance?"

"Of course. The bar is in a lot all by itself, which reduces the chance of civilian interference, but it's pretty airtight. Only one way in."

"What about his patterns? Have you been able to tail him?"

Myra shook her head. "Guy's got a bodyguard with him at all times. If I even get in the vicinity of him, he'd know. He's good. Trained professional. He'd be able to spot me from a mile away."

"I see. Do you know how to mask your spiritual energy?"

"A little. Not an expert."

"Then I'll start there. I can blend in and look human. I'll get an idea of his traveling habits and see how many demons are in his organization. Do you have somewhere you can convince your family to go for a while?"

She nodded. "Been poking the hubby about taking my son to see his grandmother in Maine."

"Good. After I do some recon, we'll send them away just to be safe and make sure they can't be used as leverage."

I sat thinking for a while. "Other than the homicidal mutt, what other weapons do you have?"

"I usually only carry a .9mm when I'm out and about, but I stay strapped in the truck. There's a rifle in a case under the seat, but I have friends out here who'll turn a blind eye if I need to borrow something heavier."

"Good. We need to get an armory going as soon as possible. We have to assume they know we want to take them out. We need to be prepared 24/7."

"You think he'll have me followed?"

"Oh, we're already being followed."

Her jaw dropped. "What?"

I gave her a flat look. "Myra, you're incredibly valuable to these clowns. Sure, no one's tailing us right this second, but they certainly monitor our movements. My guess is we'll have a welcome wagon."

"How do you know that?"

"Experience. Demons keep a wide berth around me, being associated with the archangels, but they always keep tabs in case I slip up and present them with an opportunity."

"I don't get it. Why do they want us so badly?"

"Different reasons. Some want to manipulate us into using our abilities for their cause, others want to keep us as pets, and some just think we taste good. Demons absorb our energy when we sin or when they inflict pain on us."

Myra jerked her head towards the backseat. "What about the mutt? Does he do the same thing?"

I craned my neck to look at the hellhound behind me. Ace paid me no mind. I was grateful for that. He still freaked me out. "Honestly, I haven't ever been close to one long enough to find out, what with the snarling and the whole 'murder anything that moves' deal."

"Bah," Myra said, stretching an arm out and rubbing the hound's thick, wooly mane. He licked his chops and looked at her, his deadly jaws still wide open, but this time in a happy doggy grin. "Deep down, he's all fluff. He's like the bunny from that Monty Python sketch."

I stared between the two of them. "Okay, seriously, how the hell did this happen?"

She chuckled. "Alright, I've teased you long enough. I was taking the trash out one night and I found out it was overturned and this monster was tearing it up. Of course, I got a gun to take him out, but then I saw that his back leg was effed up. He had bite marks all over him, the kind some of my cop buddies showed me before. Someone's been running a dog-fighting ring out in Houston. Looked like he'd escaped. He could barely hold himself up since he'd lost so much blood. I grabbed my First Aid kit and sedated him, then called a vet. It took her a while, but she patched him up. I set him free."

She smiled. "And he came back the next day."

I arched an eyebrow. "And he didn't try to eat you?"

"Nope. Brought me a present. A whole friggin' deer, if you can believe it. I tried to get rid of him, but night after night, he kept coming back and bringing me 'gifts.' Eventually, I gave up and started to see if he could be domesticated. Turns out he can."

"That's insane. I've never seen a hound that didn't slaughter everything it set eyes on. This is incredible."

"Don't be too impressed. He hates everyone but me and my son Chris."

I snorted. "Even your husband?"

"Hates him worst of all."

"Life is stranger than fiction."

"Ain't it, though?"

Myra's house wasn't anything like I pictured. The woman seemed to have nerves of steel and a no-nonsense air about her.

Her house was downright adorable.

It was cottage-style, with an honest-to-God rose garden on either side of the steps of the front porch. A brick wall surrounded the property — which appeared to be about four acres of land — and an immaculate black iron gate sat atop the wall dotted with a few small lanterns. The lawn was perfectly manicured, thanks in part to a tall black man currently on a riding lawnmower. When we pulled into the pristine driveway, he glanced up and smiled like Christmas had come early this year.

Myra killed the engine and hopped out, walking around to open the door for the hellhound. I got out as well as Myra's husband walked over, beaming ear to ear.

"Welcome back, babycakes," he said, catching her wrist and pulling her into a kiss.

She rolled her eyes. "I'm gonna push you under that lawnmower if you keep calling me that."

He chuckled. "Love you too, honey."

He glanced at the hellhound and nodded. "Ace."

The hound just growled at him and slunk off towards the backyard with a flick of his bushy tail. Myra's husband shook his head, still smiling. "Such a character."

He faced me. "I don't believe we've met, miss."

I offered my hand. "Jordan Amador. Nice to meet you, Mr. Bennett."

"Please, call me Charlie. What brings you to Houston?"

"Work, actually. Myra found me an opportunity I couldn't resist, so I decided to come down."

"Excellent. Will you be staying with us?"

I opened my mouth to decline the offer, but Myra spoke up instead. "Of course. The hotel rates in this town are insane. Are you all done with the lawn?"

"Just about," Charlie said, glancing to and fro. "I'll shower and make the guest room up for her."

"Thanks, babe. Where's the juvenile delinquent?"

Charlie grinned. "In his room doing his homework, like the angel he is."

"Ha! I'll believe it when I see it." She waved a hand at me. "C'mon, Jordan."

I grabbed my suitcase and hauled it up the steps as she opened the front door, spilling us into a hardwood-floored foyer. There was a flight of stairs leading down to an open door and another set of stairs to the right going to the upstairs floor. Myra went down the stairs and I hesitated, but she beckoned me and I trailed her.

Chris Bennett's room had the telltale signs of a band geek. There was a trumpet case propped up against the foot of the bed, a sliver of its golden horn peeking out in the light, posters of Louis Armstrong, Jimi Hendrix, Dizzy Gillespie, and Miles Davis were plastered to the walls, and sheet music was scattered across the carpet, both the standard measures and some with handwritten notes.

The boy wonder himself lay on his stomach with a pair of Beats headphones on, flipping through a World History textbook and writing notes into the spiral pad next to him. Myra smiled fondly at him for a second and then swatted his socked foot. He jumped and turned his head, grinning when he spotted her. His smile was all Myra, but he'd inherited his father's darker eyes.

"Sup, Mom!" Chris said, bounding up and hugging her. "Man, you got back pretty fast. Did you speed all the way here?"

"Shut up or I'll never let you practice driving the truck again."

He pouted. "Aw, c'mon, I'm getting good at it. I'll get my permit ASAP when my birthday gets here."

"Sure you will. Chris, this is Jordan Amador. She's going to be working with me for a bit and staying over with us in the meantime."

He shook my hand. "Hey."

"Nice to meet you. Love the posters."

"Thanks. So do you beat people up for a living too?"

Myra flicked him in the forehead. "Don't get smart, little boy, or I'll RKO your little behind right in front of her. What do you have for homework today?"

"Just history. Already finished my trigonometry."

"Good. I expect it to be done before a single bite of dinner passes your lips, get me?"

The boy heaved melodramatic sigh. "Yes, ma'am."

He climbed onto the bed and tugged the headphones back on, returning to his work. We left, but I found myself smiling a bit on the way.

"Cute kid," I said.

"He's a little Know-It-All," Myra said, walking into the kitchen. "Too smart for his own age. That's why I have to humble him whenever possible."

She poured us both a glass of filtered water. I sat at the breakfast nook that wrapped around the right-hand side of the kitchen and sipped, admiring the granite countertops. "What does your husband do?"

"Investment banker."

I stared. She grinned. "Yeah, I know. He's absolutely nothing like me. Total pencil-pusher. Nice and boring. The way a husband should be."

I glanced furtively at the front door. "How are you handling all the secret keeping?"

"He's used to it. All those years serving meant I wasn't able to tell him much."

"What did Chris mean about 'beating people up for a living'?"

"Oh. That. Well, my current career path is somewhat...fluid. I've been trying to find jobs that are easy to maintain or quit in the event of an emergency. Lately, I've been a bouncer. Before that, I was a substitute gym teacher. I don't like steady work, but I do need to find a steady paycheck so the hubby isn't having to hold it down on his own."

"Have you ever worked with any lost souls?"

"Not yet. Been busy trying to figure out how to get rid of Maurice. That, and following you around."

"Don't remind me," I said, rubbing my forehead. She said it so casually, as if it weren't unbelievably creepy. "Would you mind if I borrow the truck tonight?"

"What for?"

"Recon. No time like the present. I'm guessing the demons have been sitting on your house. Most demons don't recognize me on sight, so I still have the element of surprise until they circulate my picture around and figure out who I am."

"Want me to tag along?"

Again, I glanced in the direction of her front door. "No. Stay with the boys. I'll be fine."

She reached into her pocket and tossed me the keys.

"Your funeral."

CHAPTER THREE

The key to stalking a demon was not looking like myself.

For the majority of my adult life, I'd pretty much looked the same: decent enough to get a good tip at work, but no more. I was self-taught when it came to makeup, and that was an understatement. I could put on eyeliner, some foundation and pressed powder for the days when the bags under my eyes started to make me look like a raccoon, as well as some lip liner and gloss when the occasion called for it. I'd seen girls who were wizards at all types of makeup — my former best friend Lauren Yi, for example — but I was far too uncoordinated to get good at it, even with practice.

I'd also found out that I'd gotten a reputation for my clothing choices. I valued comfort and practicality above everything, so my normal wardrobe consisted of black Reeboks, blue jeans, a dark t-shirt that occasionally had something sarcastic written on it, and the too-big men's grey duster I'd inherited from Andrew Bethsaida, the Seer who saved my life. He'd been a big guy, somewhere around 6'2" with striking azure eyes and a scar in his eyebrow. The kind of guy people made a wide berth around if they wanted to keep their mouth full of teeth. I couldn't pull that off on my best day, but it did leave quite an impression with the demonic and angelic crowd alike. It made me identifiable, which was counterproductive for reconnaissance.

So I went to JCPenney.

The girl at the Sephora counter was lovely, polite, and helpful. She found me everything I needed and even things I hadn't thought about. She applied each bit of makeup in flawless movements that made me feel like a cavewoman in comparison to when I did it at home. By the time she was done, I barely recognized myself. I hadn't had occasion to get dolled up too often, maybe an event here or there to attend with Michael or Gabriel when we were still simpatico, but I'd never looked this good. Belial would've lost his mind if he could see me now.

Naturally, I had to go and ruin it.

I picked the cheapest, shortest, tightest black dress I could find in the teenager's department and squeezed into it, then took the makeup I'd bought for an unreasonable price and globbed it on top of what the girl in Sephora had done. Too much mascara, too much eye-shadow, too much lipstick, until I could have gotten a role on *Showgirls*. (My God, I can't believe I can make that reference with a straight face. I'm awful.)

The heavy makeup combined with the outrageous dress and stilettos practically rendered me invisible to the demon community, who knew only of the tomboyish cantankerous wife of their mortal enemy. No one would suspect me to be one of the only Seers on the planet Earth in this over-the-top getup. Perfect.

Now, if I could just walk in these damn platform heels without face-planting, that would be greaaaaaaat.

It took about four tries to walk in them.

Okay, five.

Six.

Don't judge me.

The Kiln was on the outskirts of downtown Houston, smartly located next to one of the major highways in case the demons needed to hightail it out of there in a hurry. The parking lot had enough square footage to make me question how large Texas really was and since it was late afternoon, there was a moderate amount of cars gathered up front. The hardcore alcoholics had probably already started coming in for their fix.

I parked Myra's truck two blocks away — tactically smart, but very unfortunate for my poor feet — and made sure my spiritual energy was buried so deeply inside me that it was undetectable. It was the only good thing about nearly being beaten to death: I barely had any to speak of anyway. That left one last little problem.

Normally, I could go into establishments without carrying a gun if my energy was at its normal levels. I could harness it like a weapon, creating invisible shards that could work like a blade, or wrap it around me like a temporary shield. With it depleted, I'd have to put on one hell of a performance so the demons wouldn't get tipped off. If they caught me, it would be hours before Myra would know to come to my rescue, and they could have me halfway across the state by then. Or, and this was a best case scenario, one of them identified me and called Belial to collect on my soul.

For a long time now, I'd kept one of the most powerful weapons I owned on my person at all times: one of Gabriel's feathers from his elegant, golden wings. It stayed in the lining of my bra as a last resort. It was powerful enough to kill any demon it touched. I could reach it easily for an attack, but it forced me to be in close quarters with my assailant. I didn't like the idea of only going in armed with the feather. I'd been using a gun with blessed bullets for most of my career as a Seer, and it made me feel itchy and uneasy to travel without it.

I sat in the oppressive heat of the truck, staring at the pearl-handled derringer in my palm. Sure, I could wear a jacket and slip it inside, but odds were they'd notice it. No choice. Just channel your inner actress, Amador. Showtime.

I took a deep breath, stashed the gun in the glove compartment, and climbed out of the truck. Then I tossed my hair a little and strutted the two blocks to the bar. The only reason I didn't fall and bust my ass was because I was humming "A Girl Like You" under my breath and that rhythm kept me in step with the heels.

A blast of cold air greeted me after I pushed the heavy oak doors open. My ludicrously high heels met with black carpet that had little bits of orange woven into it. The bar had low ceilings and equally low lighting, so everything had an unnatural glint to it that added to the motif of it being a place where things were melted or destroyed.

The bar was actually at the center of the building while the booths and tables were all set up against the walls. The bathrooms were straight ahead along with a couple of closed doors, which my gut said were probably the manager's office and janitor's closet. As I walked towards the bar, I did a brief, covert survey of the area. Twelve people in here.

The bartender looked like a cross between Kat Von D and Amy Winehouse: long pitch-black hair, nose ring, tattoos crawling up her arms, black tank top and dark jeans, and scowl that could curdle milk with one glance. She arched an eyebrow at me as I sashayed on over with a wide smile and batted my eyelashes.

"How can I help you?" she asked.

I perched on the stool, which was no small feat, and propped my folded arms on the shiny wooden bar. "Any chance you can whip up a mimosa for me?"

Her pierced eyebrow inched higher up her forehead. "Sure. Can I fetch you some caviar while I'm at it?"

I released a bubbly giggle and waved the comment aside. "Aren't you just a peach? No, just the mimosa, if you don't mind."

She lumbered away towards the freezer to fetch the orange juice. I took the time to survey what I could see behind the bar. Unsurprisingly, I spotted the butt end of a sawed-off shotgun directly beneath the section of the bar where I sat, meant to be pointed at the front door should an uninvited guest appear. An old rifle, polished to a high shine, was bolted above the hanging glasses. It had an inscription on a golden plate below it that read:

Here, perhaps
Some advantageous act may be achieved
By sudden onset, either with Hell sire
To waste his whole Creation, or possess
All as our own, and drive as we were driven,

The puny inhabitants, or if not drive,
Seduce them to our Party, that their God
May prove their foe, and with repenting hand
Abolish his own works.

It was a quote from John Milton's *Paradise Lost.* Chilling.

My entrance hadn't gone unnoticed. I felt eyes on me. Any red-blooded straight guy in the bar with a blood-alcohol content of over .08 would probably be interested, even though it was far too early to pick up girls. I'd been counting on it. I needed to know the who's who of Maurice's gang and what to expect if we were going to take them out. Demons were habitual creatures. Typically, they had a boss that they reported to, and the boss liked to have a second-in-command to handle the day-to-day things he couldn't be bothered to do. With any luck, I'd locate his second or third-in-command instead and work back from there.

Kat Von D's look-alike returned with my drink. I sipped carefully. I'd chosen it to fit my fake persona, but also to keep from tempting the slumbering alcoholic inside me. I'd never been a hardcore addict, but for a while I had a regular diet of whiskey to help me deal with my rampant nightmares. I'd been a functional alcoholic for quite some time until Gabriel and Michael helped me kick the habit, and so I didn't want to tempt fate. I hated the way champagne tasted, so it wouldn't make me backslide to have any.

"I'm guessing you're new blood," the bartender said, raking her eyes over me. "What brings you to Houston?"

I beamed at her over the rim of my champagne flute. "Fishing."

"Fishing?" she said, her disbelief clear as the glass in my hand.

"Yep. Hoping to land a big one. I'm between husbands at the moment and I need a new meal ticket. I hear this place has some good prospects, so I figured I'd stop by and check it out."

"Did you, now? Who did you hear that from?"

I winked at her. "Never reveal your sources. So tell me: what kind of fish can I land here?"

She eyed me. "You sure this is the kind of thing you wanna get into? The men out here aren't just fish. They're sharks."

"I may not look it, but I can handle myself. Where's a good place to start?" I fished a fifty dollar bill out of my wallet and planted it on the bar.

She shook her head slightly. "Don't say I didn't warn you. A bunch of these chumps are gonna start buying you drinks left and right, but if you're convinced you want to go fishing, start by saying yes to Dustin. He owns most of the pool halls in this town. He's loaded, but he's not exactly a nice man behind closed doors."

I slid her the bill. "Thanks, babe."

She snorted as she pocketed the money. "You won't be saying that in about a week. Look alive. Here he comes."

A brown-haired man sidled on up to the bar on my left with an empty beer bottle. The bartender gave him a new one without asking for payment. Bingo.

He was average height with a solid build and a square chin. By the look of things, he was mid-forties, but with that kind of Hot Dad thing going on: thick chestnut hair with a little grey at his temples, sparkling blue eyes, a five o'clock shadow, and straight, white teeth. He wore a crisp white dress shirt, Levis, boots, and a navy blazer. Houston apparently had its own version of Mike Rowe from *Dirty Jobs*. I approved.

"Now what on earth did I do to deserve to meet you?" he said, smiling wide.

"I don't know," I said, swirling the mimosa around. "Maybe saved some orphans from a burning building?"

He laughed softly. "I'm all sorts of magnanimous, huh? What's your name, gorgeous?"

"Jessica." I extended a hand and he shook it.

"Dustin. What brings you into town?"

"Oh, just here to have fun. I'm on vacation."

"Nice. Where from?"

"Atlanta."

He whistled. "You came a long way for fun."

"I hear it's worth it."

He nodded. "That it is."

Articulate, polite, clean, and well-dressed in a dive bar? I was definitely in the right ballpark. The downside to burying my spiritual energy was that I couldn't use it to detect if he was a demon or not. I'd have to try another method I'd learned from Andrew's journal.

"Well, I'm not terribly overburdened with things to do tonight," Dustin continued. "Maybe I can help you find your fun."

"Generous offer. Aren't you the Good Samaritan?"

He winked. "The best."

"Well, the Bible does say 'Love thy neighbor as thyself,'" I said, swirling a finger around the rim of the flute. It was nearly imperceptible, but I saw him wince. Demons hated Scripture. It bothered them on their most basic level. On the surface, they were human just like us, but their souls were ragged and foul beneath their skin, and the Word was like driving a stake into their soft little underbellies. Not enough to kill a demon, but it made them uncomfortable. It was basically like a demon Litmus test and he tested positive. The only question was what he ranked in their organization.

"I think I'll take you up on that offer," I continued. "Why don't you start with how you found this place?"

"Friend of mine runs it, actually," he supplied. "He's the enterprising type, which we have in common. I own a few pool halls in town. It's good money and it's not as boring as your average nine-to-five job."

"I see. Is your friend here? I'd like to leave some customer feedback."

"Well, you can always just tell me and I'll pass it along."

Aha. Maurice didn't care for solicitation. I would need to worm my way into his good graces if I wanted a shot at him. "Fair enough. You guys have a happy hour?"

"Every night from ten to two."

"Excellent. I've got another errand to run. Why don't I meet you back here around eleven and we can get to know each other a little better?"

His smile widened, and his aquamarine eyes darkened with the promise of something that would have made me nervous if I were just a normal girl. "Sounds good, Jessica. I'll be waiting with bated breath."

He caught my wrist and lifted my hand to his mouth, kissing the back of it without breaking eye contact. A lesser girl would have melted. Good tactic. Only problem was that I knew exactly what he had planned for me, which was why I decided to give myself an exit strategy so I could regroup.

I winked at him and shimmied out of the bar. Once I was back in the truck, I let out a long breath and checked to make sure no one had followed me out. The trick was to keep them from connecting the dots. I'd been wearing sunglasses when I got out of Myra's truck and so the demons watching her place probably wouldn't place me based on how I looked now. They'd assume I was just a visitor and wouldn't need to follow me around unless I presented a threat. However, if I was going to keep snooping around at this place, I'd have to take a cab, but that put me in further danger if I needed to make a quick escape. I'd gambled coming here in the truck tonight, but I hadn't turned any heads yet, so chances were low that they'd start trailing me too. I'd have to chat with Myra about getting a hotel room. The longer I stayed near her, the more suspicious they would get, and they could easily infiltrate the house to find out who I was.

After I got back on the road, I texted Myra to find out if she had the contact info of the angels in the area, and she called me instead of texting back. "How did your Honey Pot mission go?"

"I made the initial contact," I said, checking my mirrors to be sure no one from the bar was following me as I drove. "We'll see how it pans out after dark. Do you know where the local angels hang out?"

"Look, I already told you I don't want them involved. They have agendas. Rules. Sure, they claim they want to keep us safe, but they have to protect their own interests, and so do I."

I gritted my teeth. "Myra, that place is sealed up tight. It's a fortress. We can't just brute force it all. If we declare war, they'll bring a hammer down hard on us and you don't want to be there for that, trust me. We might need help on this one."

"Really? If they're so helpful, why are there demons watching my place?"

"Because it's not exactly easy to catch them in the act."

"Exactly. I'd rather not bother in the first place."

"And if everything goes south? We won't have anyone to protect your family if we both die and they have no idea what happened or why. You know better. We have to be smart about this if we want to stay alive."

"No angels. We're doing this ourselves."

"Dammit, Myra, what is your problem with them?"

"They let that maniac carve me up!"

I fell silent.

"They said they would protect me, protect us, and yet Maurice just merrily strolled his ass into my home and jammed a knife into my chest. He could have killed me. He could have killed Charlie and Chris, and they wouldn't have prevented it. The angels can't be relied on. I'd rather let hell rain down on me before I go to them for help."

It took me a moment or two before I could respond. Her voice had cracked ever so slightly when she mentioned her husband and son. She may have seemed carved out of stone, but she was still human. "Myra, I understand how you feel. The angels have let me down before, in ways I can't even describe. I don't agree with you, but for the sake of our partnership, I'll let it be for now. I'm going to make another stop and then I'll be there so we can get to work. Just consider what I've said, alright?"

"Fine." She hung up. Lovely woman. Maybe I'd be that agreeable if I ever saw the age of forty.

I ran my next errand. For the record, people look at you funny when you go to Home Depot in a tiny black dress and stilettos. Who knew?

The Kiln looked completely different at night. Some places seemed to soak up the darkness and take on its properties after the sun went down. This was one of them. Even without my usual energy, I could feel something slimy emanating from the building and oozing out into the parking lot. It also didn't help that there was a couple shagging in a convertible two spaces down from where I parked. Yep. It was going to be *that* kind of night.

As soon as I pushed the doors open, classic hard rock smashed into me. Rolling Stones'

"Welcome to the Jungle." I shot a cross look at the ceiling for a second. The Almighty had a rotten sense of humor sometimes.

The booths overflowed with people, demons and humans alike, mixed together like cocktails. The sharp scent of spilled alcohol and cigarette smoke assaulted my senses as I walked towards my stool at the bar, where Dustin was fondling a Cuban cigar. His head turned and he caught my gaze, smiling slowly as I approached, as if he'd smelled me the second I walked in. He probably had. Brr.

I was wearing the same stilettos, but this time I'd switched the black dress out for a blood-orange one instead. It popped well with my dark complexion and made me easy to spot, which was what I wanted tonight. I also had a black bolero jacket with a retractable knife hidden in an inner pocket in case things went sideways.

"Evening," Dustin drawled as I curled myself onto the stool. "Glad you could make it. This place really is better at night."

"I like it," I said, winking at the bartender. "Such a different vibe after dark."

The bartender set down a napkin. "What can I get ya?"

"White Russian."

"On me," Dustin said, reaching for his wallet, but I held out a hand.

"I appreciate the thought, but some guys think buying the drink is buying the girl. I can handle myself."

Dustin's eyebrows rose. "Catty, aren't we? I thought we were friends, Jessica."

"We're friendly," I said. "Let's just see how the night goes."

He chuckled and tucked the cigar in one corner of his mouth. "Oh, baby, we're gonna get along just fine. Follow me."

I paid for my drink and left a generous tip before following Dustin to a booth closer to the back of the bar, precisely where I wanted to be. If Maurice was here, odds were he'd pass by at some point. Plus, it gave me an excuse to check out the bar's layout.

I put the current headcount at twenty-eight: ten humans, eighteen demons, based on snatches of conversation and body language. While Dustin and I made small talk, I kept an eye on who went in and out of the bathrooms, sometimes alone, sometimes in pairs.

As for my would-be suitor, he kept his hands to himself for the first half hour, and then when I freshened up my White Russian, he inched closer until he was on my side of the booth. My heart started to give me a bit of pitty-pat action. I hadn't been near a virile male specimen in a while, and getting nervous could give me away, so I went to my backup plan: asking him about himself. Demons were terribly self-involved. He spent the next half hour bragging to me about how many pool halls he owned and how much real estate cost in Texas and pretty soon my blood pressure was nice and mellow.

At last, an opportunity presented itself in the form of a sloppy-drunk burly demon who stumbled towards the hallway and went into the women's restroom since he was too blitzed to even read the sign right. Dustin was so preoccupied with himself that he didn't see it. Perfect.

I excused myself and went in after the intoxicated demon, locking the door behind me. The bathroom had five stalls and they were all empty, since the Mr. Stinking Drunk was standing in front of the sink and peeing into it, thinking it was the men's stall. What a hero.

Mr. Drunk was about six foot one and a solid two-seventy. He had a stained white t-shirt and jean vest over wrinkled Levis and brown boots, with sandy flyaway hair that reminded me of Chris Farley. I didn't see signs of a weapon on him, but he probably had a blade on him somewhere. With any luck, I'd never find out.

I took a deep breath and told myself to remember every annoying damsel character I'd ever seen in a bad movie and channeled them all at once.

I walked around the corner and let out a shrill gasp. Mr. Drunk fumbled with his zipper and turned around, blinking unfocused brown eyes at me.

"W-What are you doing in the ladies' room?" I asked.

"What?" he demanded, and then glanced at the stalls on either side of him. "Oh. Damn. No wonder the flush wouldn't work. My bad."

His beady eyes dragged down my bare legs next. Yep. Right on schedule. He licked his lips. "Nice dress."

"T-Thanks. Look, I can see you're occupied, so I'm just gonna—" I turned to head for the door, and in less than a second, he was standing in front of it.

Apparently, he wasn't too drunk to show off his demonic side.

"Maybe you can look after me for a little bit before you go," he growled.

I backed away. "I-I don't want any trouble. Please."

"No trouble, baby," he said, stepping towards me. "I'll be quick, don't worry."

I screamed as he grabbed my arm and shoved me against the far wall. Just as he tried to yank the bolero jacket off my shoulders, the bathroom door flew off the lock. Dustin appeared behind him in a flash.

Dustin grabbed a handful of the drunk's hair and jerked his head back hard, holding a Bowie knife beneath the demon's double chins. "Marcone, you dumb, fat assbucket. This is definitely not your night."

Marcone wheezed. "W-What are you doing? She's just some stinkin' whore."

Dustin dug the tip of the knife into a pocket of fat above his collarbone and a trickle of blood slid out. "She's not a hooker, Marc. She's with me, and you just attacked her."

"N-No, I didn't, man! She came onto me!"

Dustin aimed a disturbingly calm look at me. "Jess, is that true?"

"No. The creep grabbed me after he took a piss in the sink."

Dustin clucked his tongue. "Now that just ain't gonna do, Marky-Mark."

"You can't kill me! Not on neutral ground, man!"

"It's neutral ground when I say it's neutral ground," Dustin hissed. "That doesn't count for sloppy drunks who come in here and don't know the rules. Apparently, someone needs to teach you a lesson."

His arm tensed to slit the fat demon's throat.

"Wait!" I cried.

Dustin turned his gaze on me slowly. I licked my lips.

"Let me do it."

Dustin went absolutely still. "Pardon me?"

I filled my voice with cold fury. It wasn't hard. "He thinks women are toys. Maybe it's time he learns otherwise."

The drunk squirmed, trying to wriggle free, but the older demon held him still and kept staring at me as if he'd seen me for the first time. "You sure about that? Go down this road and there ain't no turnin' back, baby."

Slowly, I nodded. "Alright."

Dustin clapped one hand over the fat demon's mouth and yanked his head to one side, exposing the rest of his neck. "Take my hand."

I settled my fingers over his, feeling the power and strength behind them. "Draw a straight line across his throat. Press forward hard. Don't let go until he stops moving."

The fat demon squealed against Dustin's hand. I felt him shaking with fear and blind panic. I could stop this whole thing right now. Walk right out. Never look back. Keep my hands clean for once.

Instead, I stared straight into Dustin's empty eyes and slit the fat demon's throat.

In movies, the blood always slid straight down in an artful, perfect line. In real life, the blood squirts in every direction. There are hundreds of places for it to come gushing out. His neck became a fountain in seconds and his muffled screams turned into gurgles that petered out in only seconds. It didn't take him long to die.

Dustin let the corpse hit the tile floor, still staring straight into my eyes, his knife, hand, arm, and shoulders as wet and sticky with blood as my own. Then he swept me up in his arms and kissed me, shoving me into the wall.

It was frantic, heated, and terrifying. I hadn't kissed anyone in months, not since Michael. Kissing my husband had spoiled me. He knew every inch of me, and how I liked to be kissed, whether it was gentle or fierce.

Dustin's rough facial hair scratched at my cheeks as he devoured my lips. I could taste the beer, the cigar, and worst of all, Marcone's filthy, salty blood. The urge to shove him away was immense, but I had to sell it or this whole act would have been for nothing. I let him kiss me for a while, until I felt the press of his arousal between my legs.

I broke from his mouth and reached for that sweet, doe-eyed damsel voice again. "Not here. Not like this. I want you, but I want it to be perfect. At the right time, you know?"

Dustin licked his lips, panting hard, and I waited to see if I had appealed to his ego. He didn't know it, but I could see him working it out in his head, if he wanted to force me to obey him or if he would let me go. I couldn't help holding my breath. Now or never. *Come on, demon. Fall for it.*

Finally, he nodded. "Yeah. You're right, baby. Not tonight. Not every girl has the balls to kill a man. I can certainly wait for a girl like you. Got that darkness in you. I like it. Don't see that a lot these days."

Some part of my soul withered at his words, but I didn't let it show on my face.

Dustin grinned and kissed me once more. "Welcome to the jungle."

CHAPTER FOUR

Unfortunately, I did dream that night.

The first part was hazy and hard to understand. Lots of yelling and fighting. I was in the middle of a brawl and icy rain slapped down on me from every angle. Flashes of light. Pain. Confusion. I just wanted to get free, but hands grabbed me in the darkness and threw me onto the soaked concrete. I gasped desperately as the rainwater and the blood in my mouth mixed and choked me. Couldn't move. Couldn't see. Could only feel booted feet kicking me in the ribs and stomach over and over again until I blacked out.

Then, like magic, everything cleared and I found myself in a lounge I'd never been in before.

The room wasn't terribly large, about thirty feet in either direction, and it was dimly lit except for a spotlight over a round table with only two chairs. Soft R&B music thrummed in the background: "Use Me" by Bill Withers. The walls were dark green. There was a red leather couch against the wall across from me and a bookshelf to the right of it. A round table sat in the center with green felt across it. I didn't see a door. Curious.

My attention diverted from the table when I heard the unmistakable sound of someone shuffling cards. I glanced up to see a man step into the circle of light from the overhead lamp. Jet-black hair, a white button up shirt, burgundy tie, navy slacks, and black dress shoes.

I sighed and massaged the bridge of my nose. "Not again."

Belial offered me his usual infuriating grin. "Welcome back, my pet."

"I take it my spiritual energy is still depleted enough that you can still creep into my headspace?"

"Your powers of observation continue to impress me."

I dropped my hand and glowered at the archdemon. "Look, I've had an extremely long day and I'm not in the mood for your bullshit."

"Long indeed, from what I gather," Belial said, bending the stack of cards between his long, slender fingers. "Your mind is cluttered with images of violence. What did the Almighty require of my favorite Seer today?"

"As usual, a big helping of none of your business. Get lost, Belial. For God's sake, just let me sleep."

"I will." He drew out a heavy cushioned chair that matched the couch and sat down, folding one leg over the other and fixing me with a satisfied smirk. "...after you play poker with me."

"Seriously?" I demanded.

"Seriously," he echoed.

"What are we even playing for?"

The smirk stretched from ear to ear, transforming into a grin. "Clothing."

I stared. "You want me to play strip poker with you."

"*Oui.*"

"Eat shit."

He offered a gallant shrug. "The faster you play, the faster I leave you alone so that you can sleep. Those are the terms, dear Jordan. Take them or leave them."

I threw up my hands, made a strangulation gesture in his direction, and finally stomped over to the table. "Fine. Deal so I can get this nonsense over with already."

Belial chuckled as I sat down. "Such a short temper, my sweet. What troubles you?"

"Aside from my sworn enemy stalking me in my dreams?" I growled, crossing my arms as I watched him shuffle the deck again. "I'm trying to exterminate a demons' nest."

"I see," he said, flicking cards down on the felt-covered table. "Not easy business. Surely you're not foolish enough to embark on this endeavor by yourself?"

"No, I've got help," I said, arranging the cards. "It's proving more dangerous than expected, that's all. It's been a while since I've had to pretend to be someone I'm not."

"And just who are you pretending to be, my dear?"

I scowled at him. "Like you."

"Oh? How so?"

"Well, you're all about seduction and lies." I slapped down the first card. "I'm just playing it the opposite way that you do with me. Men love it when you cater to their egos, and demons are like that but on steroids. It's disgusting, but it works."

"Only for simple men," he said, examining his cards before choosing. "Boys, really. I had my fill of obedient damsels by the time they were building your first cities. Complex women are far more enjoyable."

I snorted. "So you say. Don't you still want me to be the Harley to your Joker?"

"Nonsense," he sniffed. "You could never pull off a spandex suit."

I rolled my eyes. "Naturally."

"And so your damsel act is weighing heavy on your soul?"

"That's overstating it a bit, but..." I sighed. Might as well be honest. He was already in my head anyway. "Yeah. I've managed to make it this far without having to use my feminine wiles much, as you can attest to. I don't like it. It's not who I am."

"Perhaps not, but I think you're looking at the glass half-empty."

"How can I not?"

"It takes strength and fortitude to do such a thing. Not many are capable or willing. You are both. Don't think of it as sullying your name. Think of it as a challenge. Unfamiliar territory to be conquered. You'll sleep easier if you think of it from that perspective."

"Meaning that I won't be forced into playing strip poker with someone I hate?"

Again, he shrugged. "If you're lucky."

We laid down our hands. I won. It was impossible to keep a smug smile off my face.

"Sorry, demon. Looks like tonight's not your night."

"Not yet," he said, unraveling the burgundy tie from around his neck and letting it drop to the floor. Some men needed to loosen the knot first, but he did it in one smooth motion, as if he were used to undressing in front of women. Didn't surprise me in the least.

He shuffled the cards again and let me deal this time. "Have you already identified the nest's leader?" he asked.

"Yes."

"Is that your seduction target?"

"No. I'm aiming for his second banana to work my way into their organization."

He nodded once. "Smart girl. A frontal assault would be too obvious. What tactics are you considering to eliminate them?"

I eyed him. "Why are you asking? So you can sabotage it by warning them early?"

Belial rolled his eyes. "Making conversation, pet. Keeping you distracted might win me the next hand, after all."

"Their stronghold is too well-protected. I'll infiltrate and plant a charge during their next staff meeting and blow them all to kingdom come."

He nodded again. "Ruthless. I approve."

Again, I regarded him, trying to figure out if he really was just making conversation or if he had an ulterior motive. He wasn't the type for small talk. "Why are you really here, Belial?"

He flicked his reptilian gaze up at me. "I've already told you that."

"Yeah, and lying is as natural as breathing to you," I said. "What do you want? Have you forgotten the part where I promised to hunt you down for betraying me, for making me betray my husband and my friends?"

Belial tilted his head slightly and sarcasm coated his next words. "How's that going, by the way?"

I held my hand behind my back and concentrated with all my might until I felt a weapon materialize. I withdrew the retractable dagger and slammed the blade down on the table, between his first and middle finger. He didn't flinch, nor did he break eye contact with me.

"I didn't forget," I whispered. "You may be older than time, but I will find you eventually, especially if you keep poking around in my grey matter."

I let go of the dagger. He plucked it out of the table and set it aside. "I have no doubt that you will. However, this is neutral ground, so to speak. As your suitor, I am allowed visitation rights, am I not?"

"Suitor," I said in between harsh laughter. "Right. Sure. I think if I look up 'consent issues' in the dictionary, I'll find a picture of you naked."

Belial actually laughed. It was rare to see him do that instead of giving me one of those condescending chuckles. I often forgot he genuinely found me funny. "Consent in your human terms is much too simplistic. Maybe when you're older, you'll understand what it actually means."

"I'm pretty sure 'no means no' is cut and dry."

He spread his cards out on the table, smirking. "I guess we'll just have to find out, won't we?"

I glared. "Don't get cocky. It's unattractive."

I kicked my tennis shoes off. He shuffled and dealt the cards again. We played another hand and I won this one, so he took off his shirt. I pretended not to notice the way the light played off the rolling muscles of his chest, shoulders, and biceps, all pretty and gleaming like polished marble. It was all the more noticeable since he didn't have his wings out this time.

"Tell me something," I said, with less heat.

"Hmm?" he replied from around a Lucky Strike cigarette that he'd ignited with a silver Zippo lighter.

"Why do you still work for Lucifer?"

He looked at me then. "Come again?"

"You're one of the most independent demons I've ever met. Why haven't you rebelled? Why still follow orders when you so clearly have a vision of your own?"

Belial arched a thin eyebrow. "Aside from the fact that he would most certainly wipe my existence from this world if I rebelled?"

I only shrugged in reply. He smoked for a while before answering. "I have vision in spades. What I lack is simply the will to mount an insurrection against my Master. I lost a war once. It cost me my soul. I have no need to lose again."

I didn't have a response to that. It was...alarmingly honest, or at least it sounded that way. Then again, he'd always possessed this weird honesty I couldn't shake. There were times when he didn't feel like the most evil bastard alive. Sometimes I could see the tiny remnants of an actual person inside of him.

He won the next hand. I peeled off my socks. He frowned at me, having expected either my shirt or my jeans. Ha. Served him right.

"Now answer my question," the archdemon said after we started the next round. "Without your valiant husband, how long do you suppose you will last out in this nasty little world of ours?"

"Long enough," I said, slapping another card down. "I'll kill as many of your kind as I have to in order to survive. I don't need…him."

Belial watched me, inhaling slowly on his cigarette. His limpid eyes felt like the arid heat I'd experienced sitting in Myra's truck, scorching my skin where his gaze touched it. "Is that right?"

I glared. "You don't believe me?"

"Yes…and no. I saw who you were before you fell in love with your archangel. You have more than enough to survive without him. That is where he and I differ. He thought you weren't whole when he saved you. I think you are."

He blew out a mouthful of smoke and it wreathed his dark hair like dirty grey thorns. "But I also think you have set yourself on a self-destructive path by being without him and without the angels at your side."

"Pretty sure that's still none of your business."

"You," he said slowly, revealing that he'd won the hand. "…are always my business, Jordan Amador."

He extinguished the cigarette on a nearby ashtray. "Now then, what shall it be? The shirt or the pants?"

Belial smirked before continuing. "Or will you try your hardest to chicken out and wake up?"

I stared him straight in the eye and pulled off my t-shirt in one smooth motion.

Belial licked his lips and exhaled. "Lovely."

I sat forward in the chair, my elbows on the table, palm up as I reached for the cards. "My turn to deal, right?"

I wasn't terribly busty. I barely filled a B-cup, but Belial's eyes were all for my minimal cleavage as he handed me the deck. It wasn't even my turn to deal. Men.

"Last hand," I said. "Winner-take-all. You in, archdemon? Or would you rather chicken out and wake up?"

Belial chuckled. I really wish I'd been wearing a shirt, because it got a reaction out of me that it shouldn't have. Damn sexy voice. "Deal the cards, Seer."

I hadn't played a ton of poker in my lifetime, but I'd played enough to be able to build a decent hand and know when to fold. This wasn't the time to fold. I wasn't about to lose to this son of a bitch. Not tonight.

The time finally came. We didn't break gazes as we set the cards on the table. I had four of a kind.

And the son of a bitch had a royal flush.

Belial's lips curled up in a victorious smile. "It's as you said, my pet. Winner-take-all."

I went for the knife. Belial grabbed the single bulb in the lamp above us and shattered it, swallowing the room in total darkness.

Shit.

I backed away from the table and strained to hear movement or footsteps, but predictably, there were none. My heart hammered wildly against my rib cage as I stayed perfectly still, trying my best to stay calm or I'd give away my position. Dammit. I couldn't see anything. Maybe his lighter was still sitting on the table. Sure, it would give me away too, but I couldn't stab something I couldn't see.

Gently, I swept my fingertips across the table until I found his lighter. *Count of three, Amador. Get a quick look and then attack.*

Icy sweat trickled down my spine. Three. Two. One.

I flicked the lighter on. This half of the room was empty. Which could only mean—

Belial wrapped his long arms around my waist from behind and slid his mouth right up next to my ear. "Boo."

Then he blew out the flame and I was in darkness again.

Ever tried to wrestle someone in the dark? It wasn't easy. Also, it hurt. A lot.

Belial overpowered me in a handful of seconds, wrenching my arms behind my back and keeping them there with one hand on my wrists. The other he used to encircle my neck and keep me still against the wall of heat and muscle that was his bare chest. He didn't try to make me drop the dagger; he had a violence kink a mile wide so it made sense in a twisted sort of way.

"Tsk, tsk, tsk," he clucked his tongue while I continued struggling. "Someone's a sore loser."

"This is a dream," I hissed. "You could have cheated for all I know."

"Mm, good girl," he purred, nuzzling the nape of my neck. "Took you long enough to think of that. Too little too late, I'm afraid. I want my prize."

"Go to hell."

"I have a vacation home there, remember?"

"Shut up!" I hooked my ankle behind his right leg and jerked hard. We crashed to the ground in an unceremonious heap and I heard him choke sharply. Warmth and wetness slid down over my hand. Holy shit.

I scrambled for the lighter and flicked it on. Belial lay face down, his arms beneath him...and a pool of blood forming around his midsection. He'd fallen on my dagger.

"Uh," I said, stunned. "I meant to do that?"

I chewed my bottom lip and glanced around. No exits. Was I just going to wake up now? Or did killing him trap me in here until morning? I had no idea how dreamscapes worked.

"Screw it," I muttered as I knelt next to the bleeding archdemon. "Hey, you. Still alive? How do I get out of here—gah!"

Belial clamped a hand down on my forearm and rolled me underneath him with the mother of all shit-eating grins on his lips. The lighter clattered to the tiles nearby, still lit by the grace of God. "Made you look."

"Made you look?" I sputtered. "I *stabbed* you."

I jerked my chin down at the dagger currently sticking out of his lower abdomen. Dark beads of blood were still spilling out and dripping along the handle, then falling onto my bare stomach.

Belial followed my gaze and didn't seem the least bit bothered by the sharp object currently impaling him. "Well, yes, technically, but you still fell for it. Literally, in fact."

"Why don't you let me go and I'll do it properly this time?" I snarled.

Belial shuddered and leaned over me, digging the handle into my navel. "Oh, if only you would, my pet. Pain is but an aperitif to pleasure."

"You have serious issues, demon."

"So do you," he whispered, his lids lowering over his pale hellfire eyes. "You like to play with fire as much as I do. You could have tried to wake up. You chose to stay. You chose to challenge me. Some part of you wanted this outcome. I wonder why that is."

He dragged my arms up and crossed them, pinning my wrists with one hand, and with the other he reached down and pulled the dagger from his belly. I tensed as he raised the bloody blade up until the faint firelight spilled over it. "Or perhaps you should find out for yourself."

He flipped the dagger so that the handle faced me and let go of one of my arms. I frowned up at him, confused, as he slid the dagger into my hand and then brought the blade up to his chest, just below his left pectoral.

"Kill me," he whispered. "Here. Now."

"This is a trick," I said, my voice wobbly and uncertain.

"No tricks," he murmured. "You said you would find me and kill me. Here you are, up close and personal. Nothing is easier than to slip that blade between my ribs. I won't stop you."

"You think I won't do it?"

Belial smiled down at me, the fire dancing in his mad eyes. "I think you know that I've won. Either choice will give me exactly what I want."

He spread his slippery, blood-soaked fingers out until they gripped my free hand and erased the remaining inches between us. His lips were soft. Hot. Careful. Exquisite.

I woke up just as I shoved the blade through his heart.

My breath returned to me in a great, gulping gasp, as if I'd been holding it throughout the last few seconds of the dream. Minor panic fluttered through me as I didn't recognize the room I lay in. I grappled for the .38 Smith & Wesson I kept beneath my pillow before remembering I had slept over at Myra's place. Everything came rushing back to me and I forced myself to let go of the gun and settled into the pillow for a few seconds. *Calm down, Amador. Just a dream.*

I shut my eyes and slowed my breathing.

I could still feel his lips on mine.

Dammit.

I threw the covers aside and padded over to the bathroom across from the bed. The guest room was small, but comfy, with baby blue walls and hardwood floors, decorated with only one dresser and a nightstand. The blinds were drawn, but it was light out, which meant I'd actually slept through the whole night in spite of the dream.

I splashed cold water on my face a few times and dried it with the washcloth, staring at myself in the mirror. *Get it together, Amador.*

One hot shower later, I went downstairs to find Myra. The den was to the left of the staircase and as I neared it, gentle music floated up to my ears. Bells, stringed instruments holding long notes, and the faintest gurgling water.

I found Myra in yoga pants and a sports bra practicing tai chi on a mat in the middle of the den. She'd pushed the coffee table back towards the couch and put her hair up in a ponytail. She was facing the glass doors that led to the backyard and spoke without looking at me.

"Morning, sunshine. What are you doing up so early?"

"Didn't sleep that well," I admitted, watching her with interest. "Do you always get up this early?"

"Early bird catches the worm."

"Yeah, but the second mouse gets the cheese."

She faced me, smirking. "Fair enough. Well, since you're up, why don't you walk Ace for me?"

I arched an eyebrow. "Uh, because he'll kill me if I get anywhere near him?"

Myra rolled her eyes. "No, he won't. He's all bark."

"No bite?"

"Oh God, no. He'll bite you in half if you give him the opportunity. Just don't act afraid of him and he'll leave you be."

"Thanks, that's very encouraging."

Myra chuckled. "Leash is by the hat stand. He's on the front porch."

"Great. How long should I walk him?"

"He knows the way. The only reason I don't let him walk himself is because it freaks the neighbors out. Should only be about fifteen minutes."

"Fine. If I turn up missing, you'll know why." I went back upstairs, swiped my sports jacket and shades, and put on my tennis shoes before grabbing the leash by the door and going out into the crisp morning air.

It was a week day, so Charlie and Chris had already gone to work and school respectively. The neighborhood was quiet. Every so often, one of the soccer moms jogged past and threw a wave my way. Ah, suburbia. No wonder I killed demons for a living.

Ace lay on the welcome mat, breathing soft and deep as if he were sleeping, but as soon as I shut the front door behind me, he lifted his massive head and turned those blood-red eyes on me. His long ears flattened against his skull and a skin-crawling growl trickled out from between those deadly jaws. Majority of my brain screamed, "Run for your life, you fool!" but I stomped it into submission.

"Oh, stuff it," I snapped, brandishing his leash. "I don't like this anymore than you do, Cujo. It wasn't my call. Myra told me to walk you."

The hellhound kept growling. I stared at him. He stared at me. After a moment or two, he chuffed and sat up, facing forward. I spotted the little metal link on his collar and clipped the leash on. Thankfully, he didn't lurch his head around and bite my hand off. Phew.

Ace stood and shook himself, scattering little bits of black fur, and then padded down the front steps. I followed, not wanting to get my arm yanked out of its socket.

Myra's house was in the middle of a cul-de-sac. Ace led me towards the right. The houses were all roughly the same size and had nearly identical beautiful lawns and extravagant gardening. The funny part was I'd seen some dogs out in the yards when we had driven up, but as soon as Ace stepped out onto the sidewalk, all wildlife sounds ceased at once. No birds chirping, no cats meowing, no dogs barking. He was the king of the jungle, apparently. Normal people were lucky; to them, his eyes looked gold, but to animals and the supernatural community, those hellion eyes were visible and terrifying.

We walked for a while, and the longer we did, the more the hellhound appeared to relax. His ears perked up and his thick tail lifted, indicating his mood had changed. He forgot all about me as he sniffed along the sidewalk, inspecting flowers, bushes, and mailboxes, until we came to a small drainage field down the road where he decided to do his business.

On the way back, Ace's demeanor switched back to what I was familiar with. His head sunk down and he began growling at a large tree towards the corner of the block where Myra's house sat.

I frowned and guided my gaze upward at the tree. "What? Got a rogue squirrel up there, buddy?"

Ace barked twice. My heart almost stopped, it was so damn scary. He hadn't barked at anything, not once, since we were out here. Danger, Will Robinson, danger.

I checked the street. No one but us, at least for now. I let the leash go loose and Ace led me towards the massive tree, his growling growing in volume with every step. The tree was between two yards, so we weren't trespassing as we walked beneath its enormous canopy. Ace put his front paws up on the trunk and snarled at what sat on the branch nearest to us.

A cat.

"Seriously?" I said. "You dragged me over here because of a cat?"

Ace rounded on me with his red eyes, giving me the dog version of an insolent glare.

"Don't look at me like that. You're supposed to be the superdog and you just barked at a friggin' housecat."

I shook my head and started to lure him away, but then something caught my eye. I peered up at the branch holding the cat. It was just a normal-sized common housecat with short white fur.

And blood-red eyes.

Shit.

It was a hellcat.

I didn't let the recognition show on my face. Instead, I chided the dog and dragged him away towards Myra's place, pretending to still be annoyed.

Hellcats were most commonly used for one thing: surveillance. I had run into one while I was investigating Michael's supposed murder: a little black cat named Bast who had been reporting back to Belial with my movements. At the time, I hadn't known they even existed, so I hadn't gotten suspicious and it later led me right into Belial's trap.

Hellcats and hellhounds couldn't talk, but they understood everything we said to them and could communicate information in their own way. It explained how the demons had been keeping an eye on Myra without her being able to spot them. She didn't know to look for a literal damned cat.

Myra was in the kitchen pouring coffee when Ace and I came back in. "So you're still alive, I see. Congrats."

"I found out who's been spying on you," I said, tucking the sunglasses in my jacket and lowering the hood.

Myra's eyes narrowed. "Who?"

"Not who: what. There's a hellcat in a tree a few houses down. Didn't even spot it until Ace started growling."

"Good boy," Myra cooed, scratching between the hellhound's ears. The beast leaned into it and wagged his tail. My God, did it look bizarre. "So what do we do about it?"

"For now? Nothing. We can't tip them off that I'm in town. I pretended like I didn't know any better, so the hellcat won't report anything suspicious to his handlers. However, we can't assume that they'll be ignorant forever. My guess is that my new boo over at the Kiln will start asking questions after I meet up with him later. I need to move up our timeline so they don't get wise and send an actual surveillance team over to monitor you."

Myra frowned. "Moving up the timeline can be risky. If you overplay your hand, you'll tip them off."

"I know," I sighed, pouring myself a mug of coffee. "That's why I need you here. I've already written out instructions for the bomb. I need you to assemble it while I'm gone."

"Where are you going? I thought you weren't meeting Dustin until tonight?"

"I've got some recruiting to do."

Hermann Park Conservancy was probably the most fresh air I'd had since I'd broken into the Garden of Eden.

Long story.

As usual, it was uncomfortably hot, but I'd found a nice bench with some shade to sit and people-watch. Families roller-skated past and I waved back at the excited little kids who drifted by, their laughs infectious. Joggers zoomed along the winding walkway with their dogs attached to their hips. Old couples eating ice cream and holding hands wandered through the nature trails. Everyone seemed to be having a good time.

Too bad I was looking for dead people.

Seers had many responsibilities as the anointed descendants of the original twelve disciples, but the most pressing was helping restless souls find the afterlife. Sometimes when someone died, they had so many unfulfilled desires or unresolved issues that it caused them to stay anchored to the Earth to wander as ghosts. Normal people couldn't see them, but angels, demons, and Seers could. Only a select few could interact with their environment, the kind known as poltergeists, and typically it wasn't a good thing if they could. Souls deeply rooted in rage could eventually become powerful enough to be corporeal and hurt people. I'd met a couple, and they still gave me nightmares to this very day.

Searching for a lost soul in Hermann Park didn't necessarily mean someone had died here. Ghosts were anchored to places that held significant memories to them. They were also instinctively drawn to the nearest Seer, even at great distances. I'd once met a soul who walked all the way from North Carolina to Albany, New York, for heaven's sake. Poor thing. At least we'd been able to help her in the end.

Point being, if I stayed here long enough, eventually I could spot any wandering spirits in the vicinity. It also gave me the opportunity to figure out if Dustin was having anyone follow me now that I'd basically pledged to be his boo. The thought made me feel like taking fifteen burning hot showers. However, I was in the clear. No one was following me. Yet.

I checked my watch. Three hours and counting. If I didn't find someone soon, I'd be on my own for covert recon. Not a place I wanted to be, really.

I sighed and tilted my head back on the bench.

There was a man standing directly behind me.

"Shit!" I screeched, instinctively jumping to my feet.

He was around six feet tall and of Arabic descent. His black hair was thick and hung down to just below his chin, and he had an artfully trimmed goatee that reminded me of Tony Stark. His eyes were dark and sharp even under the dappled sunlight from beneath the tree. He wore a plain red Under Armor t-shirt, basketball shorts, and jogging sneakers, and had a large half empty water bottle in one hand. He also didn't react to me nearly leaping out of my own skin, which wasn't normal.

I'd been a Seer for a while. Very few people could sneak up on me, and said people were almost never human.

Still, I decided to play dumb to get a read on the guy, so I clutched my chest and muttered, "Sorry. You scared the hell out of me."

"I'm sure Belial will be disappointed to hear that," he said with a heavy Israeli accent.

I stiffened. He'd whipped it out on the first meeting. Great. Park full of innocent people. I was nowhere near an exit and I didn't have my gun. This would not end well. The only thing I could do would be to go down swinging.

"What the archdemon doesn't know won't kill him," I said carefully.

"Maybe not." He sipped the water and glanced around. "What brings you to town, Ms. Amador?"

Shit. He'd ID'd me too. "Sight-seeing."

He nodded once. "It is a lovely park, isn't it? Perhaps you'd like to go for a walk with me?"

"Sorry, but my mother taught me about Stranger Danger."

The man smiled then, revealing sparkling white teeth. "Yes, I imagine she would have. She had such potential. We were saddened at her passing."

I eyed him. "You knew my mother?"

"No, but I knew Andrew Bethsaida. He spoke well of her, and often."

I blinked. "Holy shit, man. You're an angel?"

He nodded. "My name is Jon."

~ 82 ~

I let out a tense breath. "Did you really have to scare me like that?"

He shrugged. "What is life without a little excitement?"

"Tell that to the nine lives I just lost at once." I paused, thinking. "Jon? Myra mentioned you. Are you the one who trained her?"

"Yes. Now, about that walk?" He gestured towards the trail. I fell in step beside him as we started away from the bench and deeper into the park.

"How'd you find me?" I asked. "My energy is still suppressed."

"Kismet, I suppose," he said. "I was not looking for you, but I happened to spot you during my run."

"We've never met before. How do you even know what I look like?"

"It may seem unsettling, but the angels keep tabs on any Seers who are alive and well. We keep profiles of you in case of emergencies." He paused. "Also, Gabriel is a friend. I've seen pictures of the two of you together at his home."

I shut my eyes for a second, suppressing the wave of loss and regret that welled up inside me at his words. It felt like someone had shoved a sword through my chest. Gabriel masqueraded as a philanthropist and owned literally thousands of properties all over the world. Apparently, Jon had been to at least one that had photos of me in it. Dammit.

But all I said aloud was, "Oh."

We continued walking for a little bit before he spoke again. "Are you in contact with Myra Bennett?"

I arched an eyebrow at him. "Are you asking a rhetorical question? I assume you are watching over her family, so you'd know that already."

Jon breathed out through his nose, as if he were counting to ten. "True enough. Let me rephrase. What exactly are the two of you planning?"

"Do you really want me to tell you? Isn't it better if you have plausible deniability?"

A smirk touched his lips. "In most cases, yes. In this case, no. I am…concerned for her safety. That is all."

"Why? She's more than proven that she can take care of herself."

"Yes, but she is also unbalanced by fear. You of all people know what can happen when one is faced with the sadistic choice between doing what is right and doing something to protect a loved one."

"Me of all people," I said with a snort. "It's never long before one of you brings that up."

"Ms. Amador," Jon said sharply, narrowing his eyes at me. "I do not take this matter lightly and neither should you. Whatever you have planned is dangerous and I have been charged with keeping her family safe."

I stood my ground. "She asked me to help her. Me, not you. I don't agree with her methods either, but I do respect her perspective. If you're so worried about what we're going to do, then either be proactive and stop the demons first, or stay out of it entirely. Besides, you're powerful enough to take me out of the equation if you wanted to, so why the dialogue, Jon? What do you really want?"

"I am perfectly aware that I could remove you from this situation," he said quietly, and it made gooseflesh break out along my arms. "However, that is not my way. Choice is the only thing that you as human beings are granted in this world. I will not break my rank by taking that away from you. All I can do is warn you. This is a mistake. Reconsider. She is not ready for what the two of you are about to attempt."

"Then train her. Make her ready. These monsters don't sit around waiting for us to come out of the oven like a chicken, for heaven's sake. They already threatened her family. She came to you asking for help, but you said no. What would you do if you were her, Jon? Can you look me in the eyes and say you'd just let it go?"

People passing by gave us odd looks, but made a wide berth nonetheless as we stood to the side of the path, glaring at each other.

After a moment, Jon glanced away and sighed, massaging the bridge of his nose. "You are as stubborn as Gabriel made you sound."

I almost smiled then. "He should talk. I once told him that we had a twenty-five dollar cap on all Christmas presents, and he bought me a dress that costs four hundred bucks."

Jon chuckled. "That does sound like him."

He sipped his water again. "How far have you gotten inside their nest?"

I surveyed our surroundings just to be sure I still wasn't being followed before I answered. "I've fake-seduced his second-in-command. I think I might have a shot at Maurice tonight, but that's why I'm trying to recruit someone to do it for me. I need to know if he'll be there for the staff meeting coming up."

"I can confirm he is in town, but he hasn't been sighted in a while. We think he decided to lie low after he made that threat to Mrs. Bennett's family."

"Is there any information you can share that might be helpful?"

He sighed. "This is unwise, but...I can get you the full floor plans for the bar. Do you have a pen?"

I dug through my small knapsack and brought mine out. "Write down your email address."

I scribbled it onto the back of a business card he'd given me. He pocketed it. "I will send you the plans before sundown."

He regarded me seriously. "Ms. Amador, please know that while I can offer this assistance, the angels will not be able to provide you with support if you go through with this assault. If we were to interfere, it would constitute an all-out war and we have to prevent that at all costs."

"I know," I said, and couldn't keep the bitterness out of my tone. "The needs of the many outweigh the needs of the few, yadda yadda yadda. I've seen *The Wrath of Khan*, alright?"

"I am sorry." He started to leave, but then he glanced back at me. "We will protect her family. You have my word."

"Thank you."

Jon nodded to me one last time. "Godspeed, Ms. Amador."

I watched until he was gone from my sight, lost in the forest.

CHAPTER FIVE

Jon's generous offer of the blueprints to the Kiln made me slightly readjust my plans. I took them to a print shop and had them blown up to a 24x36 print to get a better idea of what we'd be dealing with in just a couple of days. It turned out that the upper floor was indeed just a bar with nothing special about it. My hunch about the office had been right, but I didn't know that it had a trap door that led to a basement.

The basement was what gave the demons' nest its name. Demons operated in cities running any kind of sin they could get their hands on: drugs, prostitution, serial killing, human trafficking, whatever the area could supply them. Some paid off the police while others simply infiltrated it to keep the real police officers off their scent. Odds were that they kept the bulk of their stash in the hidden basement for easy access.

It pained me to do so, but I took a cab to the Kiln this time to avoid anyone identifying Myra's truck and putting two-and-two together. Since I didn't want Dustin to feel me up, I'd dialed down the strumpet costume to something more modest: a black V-neck blouse, tight blue jeans, and knee-high boots. The blouse had a plunging neckline, but I'd put a crimson tank top on beneath it, since the scar over my heart could also make me identifiable to the demons. The Spear of Longinus — yes, the same one that pierced the side of Christ — had left a nasty puncture wound that had healed over time, but the trauma still left me with the urge to cover it up even when I wasn't in the presence of evil. The angels possessed the ability to heal anything short of a mortal wound, but I'd specifically told them not to heal the scar. I needed to be reminded every day of what I had survived, what I had conquered, and what I needed to always be wary of for the rest of my life.

Dustin was waiting for me on his usual stool when I walked in. Cage's "Ain't No Rest for the Wicked" blared accusingly overhead on the sound system. The bar wasn't as crowded this time, but it was still loaded with whooping and hollering patrons sloshing their drinks. Different bartender this time; a heavily-tattooed, bald black girl around my age. Maybe that was some kind of theme for the bar.

"There she is," Dustin said, sliding an arm around my waist and all but pinning me to his firm chest. He gave me a kiss, but thankfully no tongue this time. "Been waitin' all night for you, gorgeous. How's Houston treating you?"

"Wonderfully," I said. "Even better now that I'm here."

"Well said." Dustin waved to the bartender. "Can I get a round over here? Whiskey neat."

I adopted an offended look. "Do I look like a whiskey kind of girl?"

"Aw, babe, walk on the wild side," he teased, but then something dark clouded his eyes. "After all, you didn't seem to mind so much last night."

I resisted the urge to shiver. "Be that as it may, I'm not a fan. Something lighter, maybe? Clear liquor is where it's at."

"Nonsense. You'll love it." The bartender handed him the two tumblers and he led me over to our usual corner. I tried not to drag my feet. Dammit. If I asserted too hard about the whiskey, he'd get suspicious. I also didn't want to fall back into my old habits. Decisions, decisions.

Dustin lit up a cigar and sipped his whiskey before continuing. "So about last night."

I met his gaze evenly. "What about it?"

He blew out a puff of smoke. "What's your story? Women as beautiful as you typically don't respond to violence on that level the way you did. Hell, for a second there I almost thought you weren't gonna come back, but you did."

I smiled. "Now you're wondering why."

He chuckled. "I may be as pretty as an angel, but I know I'm not enough to make a girl like you come back for seconds unless she's after something. Just what is it that you're really looking for, Jess? You're not here for a good time. Last night wasn't a good time. You got your hands dirty, and you didn't seem to mind too much."

"You're way too handsome to be this smart."

He grinned. "Ain't I just?"

I suppressed the urge to roll my eyes. Boy, he was eating out of the palm of my hand. "I've been on the road a lot. Seen some things. Bad things. Most people run from that sort of stuff, but I've always been fascinated by it. Besides, nobody crosses me and gets away with it. My hands don't always need to be clean."

"Well," he said, leaning into my side and sliding an arm around my shoulder. "To tell you the truth, my real estate ventures aren't exactly what get me out of bed in the morning. What would you say if

I were to introduce you to some people I know? You could walk away from this a wealthy woman."

"I guess it depends on what you have in mind."

"If you're up for it, we could use someone to run errands for us. Transport packages across town. They don't expect beautiful girls like you to do stuff like that. Gig is $5k for every trip."

I didn't hide my shock. "Wow. So crime really does pay?"

Dustin laughed. "Damn right it does. Only thing is, we have our own version of a criminal background check."

"Isn't that an oxymoron?"

He shrugged. "I don't make the rules. If you're seriously interested, then you meet my boss and we ask you some questions. If you pass, you're in."

"Okay. What if I don't?"

"No harm, no foul. You walk away, although I'd sure as hell be sad to see you go."

I knew enough about demons to know he was lying. The "criminal background check" was code for "make sure you're not an undercover cop or an angel." I weighed my options. The staff meeting was in 48 hours. Myra had made some excellent headway on the bomb, but it wasn't quite ready yet. Meeting Maurice tonight could make or break this plan. If he liked me, I'd have full access to their facility and I could get a bead on his movements. If he didn't, I'd be gutter trash in a heartbeat.

I lifted my glass of whiskey and held it out. "I'm in."

He clinked my glass with his. "Knew you would be."

We both took a drink. Mm, he'd chosen some top shelf stuff. Nice and smoky and rich. I rubbed my tongue against the roof of my mouth and then remembered the slippery slope. I set the glass down and put my hands in my lap so I wouldn't take another sip. "When do we meet your boss?"

Dustin checked his watch. "Should be out here in a bit, actually. In the meantime…"

He kissed my neck, his five o'clock shadow scratching the delicate skin. "I thought maybe we could entertain ourselves."

Heavens to Murgatroyd! Exit, stage left! "Not out here. Everyone can see us."

"What's wrong with that?" he mumbled, sifting his fingers into my hair to push it away from my shoulder. "Let 'em look."

I summoned up my best Jessica Rabbit impression and pulled away enough to look him in the eye with what I hoped was a sultry stare. "No offense, but what I've got is for your eyes only, big boy."

Take the bait, demon. Dustin shook his head slightly, a dangerous smirk hovering around his mouth. "God, that tongue of yours is silver. Can't wait to see what else it can do."

I winked. "You'll find out soon enough."

He let out another hearty, self-satisfied chuckle and relaxed a bit, keeping the arm on my shoulder as he finished his cigar. Phew. Crisis averted. Only another hundred to go.

A few minutes later, the door to the office opened. A dark-haired man about the size of Dwayne "The Rock" Johnson stepped out, and behind him came a black man in his mid-forties with piercing brown eyes and a little grey threaded through his goatee and hairline. The first guy held the door for him and I got a full visual of him. He wore a gorgeous navy suit that had some kind of sky-blue highlights that shifted as he moved, a striped purple tie, black dress-shirt, and black dress shoes. He scanned the area after his bodyguard gave him the okay and his eyes locked with mine before he glanced at Dustin.

"Showtime, gorgeous," Dustin said, sliding out from the booth. "That's my boss."

I followed him over to the two men. The bodyguard didn't even spare me a glance, and that told me all I needed to know about him. The man behind him cast a cool look over me, not quite interested, but curious nonetheless.

"And so it emerges," Dustin said. "How's the paperwork, Maurice?"

"Flat and lifeless, like your love life."

Dustin grinned. "Joke's on you, old man. Meet Jessica. She's auditioning for us."

"Is she now?" Maurice asked.

I held out my hand. He ignored it and stepped close to me. He cupped my chin in his hand and squinted straight into my eyes. Taken aback, I stood still, holding my breath.

"She's a live one, at least," Maurice concluded after a few seconds, letting me go. "No track marks, not a full-on alcoholic like your last few fancies. Is she ready to be vetted?"

"Ready as she'll ever be."

Maurice snapped his fingers and pointed inside the office. "You. In. Now."

It was decided. I definitely didn't like Maurice. However, I ignored my bruised ego and stepped into the office as I was ordered.

The blueprints had given me the square footage of the room and the location of the trap door leading to a short stairwell into the basement. It was hidden behind a fake display that made it look like a floor safe. The walls were lined with bookshelves and Maurice's expensive mahogany desk sat towards the far left wall, stacked with folders. There was an expensive bottle of scotch with two glasses on the corner of the desk next to a note that said, "With love, Barbara." Behind the desk sat an extravagantly comfortable looking chair while two plain cushioned ones were on the other side of it.

The three men filed in after me and shut the door. The bodyguard locked it. Oh joy.

"What's she auditioning for?" Maurice asked, taking his seat at the desk.

"Courier," Dustin said, plopping down on one of the other chairs.

"And why should I humor you?"

"Well, you heard about Marcone last night, right?"

"Yeah, what about him?"

"She slit his throat."

Maurice regarded me again, but this time with actual interest. "Bollocks."

"Hand to metaphorical God. I watched her do it."

Maurice kept staring. I sat perfectly still, impassive as a Tibetan monk. He stroked his goatee for a few heartbeats and then sat forward, folding his hands and resting them on the desk.

"Alright, my lil bird. Let's pretend for a second that I believe you. What's your interest in our organization, eh? What's in it for you?"

"Dustin led me to believe this position could be lucrative," I said. "I need to build a new nest egg."

Maurice smirked. "Nice pun, but pretty talk won't get you everywhere, love. I'm gonna ask you a few questions."

"You're not going to hook me up to a lie detector, are you?"

"I am the lie detector." He nodded to the bodyguard behind me. I heard the click of metal. He'd cocked a gun at my head. Fantastic. No pressure.

"Are you now or have you ever been associated with the police?" Maurice asked.

"No."

"How many crimes do you think you've committed in the last five years?"

That took me a second. The sad part was that I didn't have to lie about it. "Probably six or seven."

"Misdemeanors or felonies?"

"Few felonies, couple misdemeanors."

"Have you ever been to jail?"

"No."

"Did you come here with the specific purpose of employment?"

"Yes."

"Were you referred by any specific person?"

"No."

Maurice smiled a bit. "Good performance so far. Heartbeat's nice and even. Steady eye contact. You've done this before, haven't you?"

"If you're asking if this is the first time someone's pointed a gun at my head," I said. "Then no, it's not. I've lived a hard life. Comes with the territory."

"I like your nerves, at least. If necessary, are you prepared to protect our investments with your life?"

"Yes."

He pointed at me. "There. That's the one. Explain why you lied to me."

Shit. I took a deep breath. The easiest way to beat a demonic lie detector was not by lying harder, but by reaching for something closer to the truth. "No offense, but I didn't work this hard and risk this much just to die for some drugs. I will protect your investments with my life, but I have no intentions of dying here in Houston, Texas."

"Interesting. Where would you prefer to die?"

"Among friends and family as an octogenarian."

Maurice smirked. "Wouldn't we all? Are you running from something?"

The question nearly startled me, but only because I realized the answer. "Yes."

"Is whatever's chasing you likely to find you?"

I frowned. "Not if I can help it."

"Would it impede our business if you were to be caught?"

"No."

"Have you ever been tortured for information?"

Images of the archdemon Mulciber slicing up my back flashed through my mind. She'd been toying with me, using me to make Michael crack while he watched helpless on the sidelines. She'd asked if I thought it cruel that God would let me die defending him. Not hard to twist that into a type of interrogation, really. "Yes."

"Did you give up the information?"

"No."

"Are you afraid of death?"

I thought about the Spear of Longinus plunging into my chest and the pain exploding through me like an acid bomb. I thought about the fear and regret on Michael's face when I told him to let me go so that he could return to being an archangel. The tears running down Gabriel's pale cheeks as he kissed my forehead. I couldn't go through that again, and maybe I never would, but it was all a lie. The average Seer didn't live to see the age of fifty, not if their Awakening happened before that time. Some had been fortunate, but most were casualties of the war between heaven and hell. What did my life matter? I was just another soldier. I wasn't welcome on either side of the battlefield.

But was I still afraid to die?

Someone pounded on the door. Maurice nodded to the bodyguard, and he opened it. Some woman I didn't know—maybe one of the barmaids—stood there, out of breath, and I could hear crashing and angry voices behind her.

"Someone's started a damn bar fight. Can you come break it up?"

Maurice sighed. "Sometimes I really regret our occupational choice for this place."

Dustin grinned and cracked his knuckles as he stood up. "Name of the game, I'm afraid. Let's go bust some heads!"

"Not so fast," Maurice said. "Why don't we let our new recruit handle it?"

Dustin and I both did a double take. "Uh, what?"

"Well, she needs to be capable of taking care of herself. Prove her worth, as it were."

"She already did," Dustin insisted.

"She convinced you," Maurice said, steepling his fingers. "Not me. Go on then, love. Silence the rabble and you're in."

I pictured chopping off Maurice's head and mounting it on the wall of his office. Instead, I stood up and nodded to him without breaking eye contact. "Sure thing, boss."

I pushed past the barmaid and the bodyguard. I could hear Dustin protesting to Maurice about "breaking his new playboy bunny before he even had a chance to play with it." I couldn't blame him. Well, yes, I could, but he had a point that it was pretty messed up for Maurice to ask a hundred-and-twenty-pound girl to break up a demonic bar fight.

Guess it was a good thing I'd been in one before.

Bar fights, in my experience, were only more violent versions of food fights. No main focus, just things being thrown in every direction. Whether it was a knuckle-sandwich or a real sandwich, at first glance, it was pure chaos. However, to someone who was in life-or-death situations on a weekly basis, I knew where to look for how to end it quickly.

Ducking a half-full pitcher of beer someone chucked, I wiggled between the men slugging each other on the hardwood floor and the women scratching and pulling each other's hair by the bar until I reached the spot where I'd been sitting before. The bartender was standing there with a scowl on her face, making sure no one got cheeky and tried to steal a drink during the brawl. She gave me a confused look when I lifted the stool over the bar and then climbed onto it.

I plucked the rifle from its perch and checked the barrels. As I suspected, it was a fully functioning weapon on display. Remington Model Eight. Good condition. Not bad for a seedy bar. It'd be a shame to lose it after I blew these scumbags to the moon in two days.

I motioned to the gun and the bartender grinned as she understood. She opened a drawer and handed me a couple of shells. I loaded the rifle, checked to make sure the barrels were unblocked, and then cocked that bad boy. I kept it tight to my shoulder and pointed it straight up at the ceiling.

Then I squeezed the trigger.

The sound was a cavernous explosion.

Dammit, was I going to have a headache later.

Despite my ringing ears, the reaction was immediate. Every demon and human still in the bar froze and locked their eyes on me.

I smiled sweetly and asked, "Now that I've gotten your attention...knock it off or I knock *you* off."

Dead silence.

Then, gentle snickering. A stringy sandy-haired man stood and wiped blood off of his chin, aiming a skeptical glare at me. "You ain't got the balls, sweetheart."

I swung the barrel and shot him in the foot as soon as the condescending epithet left his greasy mouth.

"Shit!" he roared, collapsing on his back and nursing the injury. On the off-chance he was a human, I'd actually aimed slightly to the left of his entire foot, meaning it wouldn't take off all his toes. The buckshot had skimmed the top of his foot instead; painful, but not deadly. Still, the rest of the drunken degenerates wouldn't know that.

The bartender handed me another two shells and I loaded them. "Anyone else?"

The bar patrons mumbled, "No," and regretfully started turning the chairs and tables back upright. One guy dragged the injured man away for medical attention. Some shuffled out the door now that their fun had been ruined while others settled down to finish their drinks. I winked at the bartender and replaced the rifle on the mantel before heading back towards the office.

Maurice still looked like his usual expressionless self, but Dustin seemed to be suppressing a marriage proposal judging by the smitten grin and the missile silo he was packing in his jeans. Boy, oh, boy. Could I pick 'em or what?

"That," Dustin purred. "Was the sexiest goddamn thing I've ever seen."

I flashed him a smile, but focused my attention on Maurice. "So how'd I do?"

"Very tactical," Maurice said. "How'd you know the gun would work?"

"This looks like a rough crowd. I had a hunch it was real in case of emergencies."

He nodded. "Good hunch. Alright, lil bird, you're in for a trial period. If you perform your first task to my satisfaction, we'll induct you."

He started to go back in the office, but paused. "Oh, and the holes in my bar are coming out of your first paycheck."

He and the bodyguard shut themselves back in the office. Dustin swept me up in a victorious bear hug and spun me around.

"Gorgeous," he said after he set me down. "You better start picking out the China. Every time I think I've got you figured out, you keep surprising me. Can I buy you another drink?"

"As long as it's not whiskey, sure."

He cackled and dragged me to the bar. I ordered a beer this time, since most beer was gross and would allow me to nurse it without him getting wise. Plus, it inspired him to get one as well, which actually helped my backup plan.

Impressing Maurice was good for the overall scheme, but bad for my seduction target, because now all Dustin could think about was getting in my pants. Luckily, I'd stopped by the drug store and had found a tasteless liquid laxative that I put into a small stopper tucked in the lining of my boot. He went to use the bathroom and I squirted it into his bottle. He came back and wrestled me onto his lap to make out. Thankfully, the stuff was fast-acting and so before we got past first base, it took effect. As soon as he made his second trip, I snuck out of the bar and took a taxi to my new hotel room. Dustin texted the burner cell phone I kept on me about twenty times during the fifteen minute ride. I told him I had a friend I was meeting for drinks and he sent me about thirty sad emojis before giving up.

The three grand Myra had promised me for helping her clear out the demons' nest would be collected after it was done, so for now I had to slum it with the hotel I'd chosen. I tried to stick to three-star hotels for hygiene reasons, but I could stoop to a two-star in a pinch. Hell, I'd been in roach motels before traveling with Belial, the rogue angel Avriel, and Juliana not long ago, so this place was a step up from that, at least.

The alcohol I'd consumed began to show as I shuffled in a crooked line from the door to the bathroom to start scraping off the pounds of makeup for my hot girl disguise. I took a boiling hot shower, brushed my teeth for five straight minutes and gargled a large amount of Listerine, and then collapsed onto the lumpy bed in my underwear.

I had just cuddled up with a pillow when I remembered my current chronic problem: Belial, stalking me in my dreams. Shit.

Groaning, I rolled onto my back and dragged my hands down my face. "Stupid horny bastard. I swear, if I find you, I'm gonna stab you right in the —
"

I was out before I finished the sentence.

I dreamt of a beach with white sand as fine as powder and rolling waves that were as blue-green as my estranged husband's eyes. The sun was high overhead. Palm trees waved hello to me on either side of my little lawn chair. I stood just out of reach of the shore in a red string bikini. Not really my color or my style, but it was comfortable and there wasn't anyone else here to see me anyway.

I inhaled the salty sea scent and waded into the warm water, giggling as it splashed against my knees and tickled my calves. I checked the horizon. No land in sight, no boats, no nothing. Just a private island for me and me alone. Marvelous.

I waded waist-deep into the water and shut my eyes, listening to the crashing waves, the birds squawking, and the wind whispering through my hair. I could do this for hours, days even. Nothing calmed me like the ocean.

After a while, I returned to my little chair, sipped the frozen margarita perched on the arm, and sun-bathed. I hadn't felt this relaxed in ages.

The scent of something delicious drifted past my nose. Mm, smelled like roasted pork, maybe. I sat up and turned to see that there was a little hut behind me with a whole pig on an automatic spit and a little table with other kinds of food on it. Well, it explained where my drink had come from, at least.

I went to the buffet table and grabbed some fresh pineapple, mango, and strawberries, then a few slices of pork before heading back to my chair. The pork was so succulent that the juice ran down my fingers and chin. It was worthy of the Food Network, it was so damn good.

I finished my plate and settled down to take a light nap.

I wasn't sure how long I'd been there before I heard the sand behind me shift and the sunlight on my face cooled. I opened my eyes. An umbrella had appeared. Huh. Odd.

"See?" Belial said, poking his head over into my vision from behind me. "I told you I wasn't always bad company."

I shut my eyes again. "Shit."

The archdemon clucked his tongue. "Such naughty language is quite unbecoming of you, dearest Jordan."

I glared at him as he sidled up next to me with his own chair. Angry as I was, it was bizarre seeing him in something other than a ridiculously expensive suit. He wore dark green swimming trunks and had his silky hair pulled back into a knot at the top of his skull. His skin was pale as alabaster and bounced the sunlight off his carved pecs and cobblestone abs. His upper body was smooth and perfect enough to make my fingers itch with the urge to touch it.

"Do you remember the part where I killed you in our last dream together?" I demanded. "Do you want me to drown you this time?"

"Why ruin such a perfect view with a dead body?" he asked cheerfully, lowering himself into the chair after adjusting his own large umbrella over it. "Maybe later. I'm not in the mood to get frisky just yet."

I facepalmed. The man referred to murder as "getting frisky." He was going to drive me insane one night at a time. "So you set this dream up?"

"I figured you could use a change of pace. You're terribly wound up most of the time. The beach can make even the tightest ass unclench."

He sent me a flirty smile and waggled his eyebrows. "Not that I'd ever complain about yours."

I rolled my eyes. "And what stupid nonsense do you have planned for me this time?"

"None at all. No ulterior motive. Just a beach."

"Bullshit."

"You don't have to believe me, my pet. I'm not going to do anything to you that you don't want me to."

"That'll be a first," I growled, sipping my margarita. "Is this how you court other women? Incessantly follow them around until they kill you?"

"No. You're the only one who has ever resisted me for this long. It's never been necessary. The women I seek aren't so blindly ignorant of their own desires."

"What makes you such a damn expert on women's desires?"

He arched an eyebrow. "Remember the part where I'm several million years old?"

"Yes, because clearly you can just generalize all women."

"Not all women. Women I am attracted to."

"So you don't care that it's not mutual?"

He lowered his eyelids a bit. His lashes were long. The look made me shiver a bit. "I seem to recall it being very mutual in that hotel room a few months ago. Or was it perhaps my imagination that you were moaning into my mouth while I kissed you?"

I stood then. "Do us both a favor and go fuck yourself."

For once, he didn't follow me. I stalked to the other side of the island and leaned against one of the palm trees, trying to quell my anger. His words had buried themselves under my skin like the creepy scarab beetles in the Mummy movies. What did he know? He was an arrogant pretty boy who thought with his glands. He didn't know me. He didn't know what I wanted. Who I wanted. To him, I was just something to be conquered. A trophy. What if he never stopped this game we were playing? Would I spend the rest of my life plagued with these idiotic scenarios where he manipulated me? When would they end?

I took a deep breath as the thought made me cold from head to toe. No. It wouldn't be forever. It was only because I had suppressed my energy to remain undercover. As soon as I was back to full strength, I could fight this — fight him — and everything would go back to the way it was. Then again, I had chronic nightmares, so maybe not.

When I opened my eyes again, Belial was standing in front of me with a halved coconut in one hand. I didn't jump out of my skin like I had done before. I knew he would find me eventually.

He drank from the coconut and then handed it to me. I thought about throwing it in his face, but there wasn't much of a point. Plus, I actually was thirsty. I drank it and handed it back.

There was a little cherry stuck to the rim of the coconut with a toothpick. He plucked the cherry free and held it up to my lips, staring straight into my eyes. I opened my mouth and let him slide it over my tongue. He pulled his hand back and licked his thumb where it had brushed my lower lip.

"Do you know why I am doing this?" he asked quietly.

I shook my head as I chewed the sweet fruit.

"Why do you think I am doing this to you?"

"It's all a game to you," I answered. "My life, your life, everything is just a game. You're immortal, as far as either of us can tell, so what do you care about the consequences?"

Belial made a harsh, guttural sound in his throat and tossed the empty coconut aside, muttering something in Latin that I couldn't catch. "How long have we known each other and yet you are still this dense."

"There's nothing dense about it," I snarled. "I'm not yours, Belial. Get that through your head. I don't need to know anything about you except how to kill you."

In a flash, his hand was fisted in my hair and I was pinned between the hard, hot wall of his chest and the rough bark from the palm tree behind me. He stared down at me with his serpent eyes and I could see the fury swirling around in those icy depths.

"I should kill you," he whispered, his breath hot on my cheeks. "Why haven't I killed you yet? It would be so unbelievably easy. Human bones are so brittle. All it would take is the slightest amount of pressure to snap this beautiful neck of yours."

"Then do it," I murmured. "Do it or leave me the hell alone."

"No, that would be much too quick," he continued as if I hadn't said anything. "Maybe strangulation instead. I could watch those last few gasps of air before the light dimmed in your eyes. It's troublesome, really. Living with the fact that I could snuff out your life any time I want and yet I can't stand the thought of anyone else laying a finger on you."

I frowned up at him. He stared back at me, and the anger in his features retreated to give way to something disturbingly human: concern. "That's it. Put the pieces together, Jordan."

I licked my lips, my voice cautious. "Are you…angry that I almost died?"

"At long last," he said, sarcasm thick on every word. "She has seen the light."

"How is that even possible? You've killed me yourself, you impossible asshole."

"Precisely," he said. "I killed you. No one else. Do you realize how reckless you've been with your own life, Jordan? How you've gambled, how you've been lost in this game? How lucky you were to survive?"

"What does it matter? I'm just a Seer—"

He reached up with his other hand and punched the tree in half.

I froze, scared shitless as I heard the enormous thud of its trunk collapsing in the sand behind us. His breathing came out in a hiss as he glared at me from mere inches away, practically vibrating with rage.

"You are *not* just a Seer. You are human. You are a person. Your actions have consequences that can just as easily tip the balances of this world's scales as mine can. Now do you understand why I have done this to you?"

I swallowed to wet my dry throat before answering. "You're trying to teach me to be more careful, more mindful of my surroundings."

"Yes," he said slowly. "I am. I may be a demon, but I am not without a creed. You may be alone now, but it is no excuse for being careless. If we are to ever settle our account, you will need to still be alive by the time I find you or you find me."

I shook my head. "I don't know that any of this is real. It could just as well be my imagination as it could really be you."

"That is also true. After all, chances are that you won't even remember most of this within a few weeks. The mind is a labyrinth. However, right here, right now, you will hear me out. Stop moping over what you've lost and consider what you still have."

"Like what?" I sneered.

"Life. That is all you need. That is all that any of us needs, regardless of how we choose to live it."

I wanted to shake off his words like I could shake off his sexual advances, but it wasn't as easy this time. I'd thought he just wanted to screw with me, both literally and figuratively, but as much as I hated to admit it, he did have a point. I hadn't been as careful as I'd been in the past. Bridgett shouldn't have caught me. Losing Michael and Gabriel and any semblance of my former life had affected me more than I thought. Can't believe it took Belial of all people to remind me of how dangerous the world could be if I had nothing to live for.

"Fine," I said after a while. "I get it. Don't expect a thank you."

He smirked. "It wouldn't be your style."

Without him scaring me half to death, I realized I was still pinned to the tree and he was still pressed down the length of my body. Naturally, he noticed me noticing him and settled his hands on what remained of the tree trunk, trapping me between his muscular arms. My heartbeat fluttered erratically. Too little clothing, too much skin, not enough common sense. I had to bail or I'd do something inadvisable.

"Why, Jordan," the archdemon purred. "Your cheeks are red. Have you gotten a sunburn?"

I glared. "Refer to the earlier 'go fuck yourself.'"

"Only if you promise to watch," he teased, tugging at the neat little bow on one side of my bikini.

I slapped his hand away. "Pervert."

"I prefer the term 'lecherous,' thank you very much. Besides, you're being exceptionally stubborn right now. You just admitted that it's possible your own psyche conjured me up. If that's the case, having incredibly rough, but utterly satisfying sex with me right now wouldn't be cheating so much as masturbation."

"Oh, for heaven's sake, you—"

He kissed me. His lips tasted like coconut water and tequila and sweetness and it sent jolts of sensation straight down the front of my body. My legs unconsciously parted and he took full advantage

~ 110 ~

of the movement, easing himself between them enough to roll his hips into mine. Blind pleasure simmered through me. I couldn't think straight. The kiss had completely addled my brains.

He reached up and grabbed another handful of my hair, pulling my head back and slipping his tongue past my lips. His other hand glided up my waist, my side, sliding behind me. The bikini top slackened around my chest and he broke from my lips enough to sink down towards my — *oh my*.

The fevered touch of his lips and tongue made me grip any part of him I could touch, trying to rein in my neglected libido, but all it really did was give me the chance to feel just how much of that fantastic body I'd been missing out on. Dammit, Amador, he was pure evil. He was a lying, murdering sack of shit. He was…really, *really* good at what he was doing to my breasts right now.

"Watch out!"

Betty Hutton's brassy voice rescued me from the dream.

I blinked up at the cracked ceiling of my hotel room as the big band sound of "It's a Man" shook me out of the naughty beach scene that I prayed was just my own twisted fantasy and not actually the real archdemon Belial. If it was, I'd never live that down.

I slapped my burner cell phone silent and glared at it. That had been Dustin's ringtone. Why the hell was he calling me?

It rang again and this time I rolled onto my belly and answered it, not hiding my disgruntlement. "What?"

"Got a job for you, gorgeous," Dustin said. "Interested?"

I scraped the layers of hair out of my face and tried to think straight after my disorienting dream. "Depends. Is it what you described before? Just transporting something?"

"Yep."

"Wow, that didn't take long."

"Yeah, we work fast. What do you say?"

If I could have frozen time, I would have. I wanted to think it over. Damn him for springing this on me. If I said no, he might get suspicious and think I was squirrely. If I said yes, I could get myself arrested by the cops and rot in jail while Myra would be forced to do Maurice's bidding, or worse, end up dead. If I stalled, he might think I was yanking his chain the whole time and revoke my invitation to their organization.

I shut my eyes and bit the bullet. "I'm in. When and where?"

"One o'clock. Meet me at the Kiln..." He paused, and something purely masculine slid into his deep voice. "Or I could come over now and entertain you for a couple hours, then drive you over."

I had to give it to him; he wasn't half-bad at seduction. "Thanks, but I can manage. Plus, I need enough time to get all pretty for you. See you at one, okay?"

"Can't wait, baby." He hung up. I collapsed onto the bed and let several foul, creative curse words fly out of my mouth. Talk about bad timing. This operation was getting worse by the minute.

I forced myself to sit up and called Myra. "What's up?" she asked.

"We've got a minor setback in our plan. Dustin wants me to run some product across town. What are you doing around one o'clock?"

"Still working on the You-Know-What," she said, which meant that her husband Charlie was within earshot. "But I can help if you need me to."

"It's risky, but all I need you to do is hang around the outskirts of the area in case this is some sort of trap. From what I understand, I'm basically just a drug mule. It should be quick, but if I'm not out within a certain amount of time, I may need you to create a distraction to get me out."

"Roger that. Text me when you get there with the address they give you."

"Actually, that won't work. They'll probably confiscate my phone to make sure I'm not an undercover cop. I'll have someone else deliver the message to you."

"Who?"

I smiled. "My dead guy."

CHAPTER SIX

Considering the fact that I'd be committing a crime shortly, I dressed for efficiency: soft, knee-high boots with hard soles, comfortable dark wash jeans, a plain black V-neck t-shirt, and a lightweight jacket. I would have gone for a leather jacket, but it was way too hot outside for that. I piled on the makeup as per usual and thought about tucking a knife into one of the boots, but I had a hunch that they were going to pat me down and I didn't want it to get confiscated. I also tugged my hair up into a ponytail and let it naturally curl on its own instead of using the flat-iron. I'd found that bad guys didn't play fair, and they loved to grip a big handful of my hair during a fistfight if possible. The ponytail prevented them from getting as much if they reached for it. I didn't want bald spots after a tussle.

This time, I let the cab drop me off in front of the bar and strode straight through the double doors, giving a passing nod to the bartender as I headed towards Maurice's office. The same bodyguard from last night was there and he motioned for me to turn around. I obliged and he did a quick, professional pat-down before letting me in.

Maurice sat at his desk with a pair of rimless reading glasses on his nose, shifting through papers. Dustin lazed about in one of the chairs opposite, blowing smoke rings at the ceiling. Both glanced up as I walked in. Maurice still looked unimpressed, contrasting how Dustin was shooting heart-lasers out of his eyes at the mere sight of me. Boy, had I done a number on him. I wasn't going to miss the attention after I blew him to smithereens.

"Welcome back," Dustin said, rising enough to give me a kiss. I kept my stride so he couldn't pull me into a French one and took the seat next to him.

"Alright, where am I headed?"

"You're going to be delivering some crates over to the Columbian restaurant a few blocks away," Maurice said, switching his gaze back to the paperwork. "Once you arrive, you will give them the crates and they will pay you. That's it."

"Sounds easy enough. How much money should I be expecting?"

"Two hundred thousand."

I whistled. "Makes me wish I worked off of commission."

Maurice's lips twitched upward. "Do your job well and someday you might."

"Am I meeting with anyone specifically?"

"No. Just tell them it's from Maurice at the Kiln and you shouldn't have any problems. Get changed into that—" He pointed to the navy coveralls folded on the corner of his desk. "—leave your cell phone, and Dustin will show you to the truck and give you the address."

I saluted him, scooped up the coveralls, and placed the burner cell on his desk. "Leave it to me."

He narrowed his eyes at me. "Fly straight, lil bird. Or I'll clip your wings."

I smiled, and made a concerted effort not to make it vindictive. "Will do."

The bodyguard let us out after we knocked and Dustin led me back out front where there was a large white transport van waiting by the front curb. I wrestled into the coveralls and followed him around to the rear of the van.

"Hand truck's there," he said. "Exactly four crates. Easy as pie."

"Is there some sort of manifest in case anyone asks?"

"Yep, it's upfront on the passenger's side."

"Directions?"

"Left out of the parking lot. Six lights down, then turn right and it's on your left at the corner."

I eyed him. "This isn't some sort of weird test, is it?"

"You think too much, Jess. Sometimes it's just that easy." He leaned in and kissed me again, waggling his eyebrows. "Drive safe, gorgeous."

I climbed into the van. It coughed to life, rumbled mutinously, and then allowed me to maneuver it away from the front of the bar. I squeezed the wheel between my fingers and took slow, even breaths, resisting the urge to mutter sarcastic comments to myself. There was a good chance this van was bugged, either by the demons or by whomever was watching them. It had occurred to me that their usual courier might have died during one of these "deliveries" and that was why I got the job so quickly. The thought hung over me like a fat, grey storm cloud. I was just racking up the bad karma this week.

So, of course, two lights away from the restaurant, a police car pulled up next to me.

Cold sweat instantly popped up along my spine. I kept staring forward at the stoplight. There were two cops in the vehicle, both wearing sunglasses. The one closest to me glanced over casually and I briefly panicked, wondering if I should wave or if that made me even more suspicious. Guilty? Who? Me?

Screw it. I waved. The dark-haired plain-clothes cop waved back. The light changed and they drove off. I let out a hissing breath of relief and kept going. Maybe Dustin had been right. Sometimes it was just that easy.

Ha. Yeah, right.

The restaurant had a gorgeous storefront — pale yellow with dark red trim and beautiful hand-painted murals over the sign. I shifted into Park and climbed out with the manifest. There was a key clipped to it that unlocked the back. I stacked the four crates onto the hand-truck and lowered it with the lift before rolling inside.

It was cool and dark inside, a blessed reprieve from the sticky Texas heat. The maître'd was tall and had a handlebar mustache.

"How can I help you?"

"Delivery from Maurice at the Kiln," I said. "Where should I drop it off?"

He pointed directly behind him to the swinging doors down the hall. "The kitchen is through there. Someone will sign for them and then pay you."

"Thanks." I rolled the crates down the hall and into the bustling kitchen. Among the various cooks and servers, there was a short Hispanic man with a clipboard in his hand shouting orders in Spanish to different scurrying employees.

"Hi there," I said brightly, not sure what to expect. "I've got a delivery from the Kiln. Maurice sent me."

The man eyed me. "And you are?"

"Jessica. I'm new."

"Clearly," he said, raking his brown eyes over me. "Follow me, *morena*."

He led the way through the kitchen counters until we reached an office on the right hand side of the hallway. He opened the door for me. I took a quick stock of where I was and where the nearest exit was—two doors down on the right—and wheeled the crates inside.

There were two other men already inside the office, laughing and chatting with each other. Cigarillo smoke clouded the ceiling. I was pretty sure staying in here for more than ten minutes would result in lung cancer.

The first man sitting in a cushioned chair was tall, but had to weight upwards of three hundred pounds and had glasses sitting on the edge of his nose. The second man was the most handsome of the group, with thick hair carefully brushed back from his face, an infectious smile, and a muscular frame. He and the seated man were in business casual clothing—button up shirts, jeans, and boots. Both had .9mm handguns tucked at their sides. Great.

The short man shut the door. The second he did, all the noise from the kitchen went silent. Sound-proofed office. That didn't bode well for me.

He stepped in front of me, telling the other men, "*¿Esperaba un envío?*"

I kept my face blank, but I spoke both Mexican and Castilian Spanish. He'd asked the handsome man if they were expecting a shipment.

"No," Handsome Guy replied. "*Que es?*"

"*Cerveza,*" Short Guy said, and then squinted at one of the crates on top. "*Y heroína.*"

Maurice and his low-life gang were heroin dealers. Good thing they had it coming.

Fat Guy nodded to me. "*Y la chica?*"

"*Ella es nueva.*"

"*Hermosa,*" Handsome Guy said, smirking. He pushed off from the wall and offered his hand to me. "What's your name, *morena?*"

"Jess," I said, shaking it. I half-expected for my hand to come back covered in slime. All three of them gave me a bad vibe, drug-dealers or not. The hairs on my nape stood up just looking at them. Things had happened in this room—bad things, things no one should ever have to go through. I didn't need spiritual energy to sense it. The notion practically dripped from its very walls. I needed to get out of here, and soon.

The short man reached into his pocket and withdrew a stiletto blade. I fought the urge to flinch, but he just pried one of the crates open, removed a few beers, and then pulled up a small panel on the lining of the box. His hand came away with a black plastic square about the size and weight of an ice cream bar. He tossed it to the Fat Guy, who glanced it over and nodded wordlessly. Handsome Guy started unloading the boxes and stacking them against the adjacent wall, pulling the heroin packets out of them one by one.

"I assume you want payment?" Short Guy said, walking over to the desk and unlocking it with a key ring from his pocket.

"That's what they told me," I said, trying to sound carefree.

Short Guy set a large grey metal box on the desk and opened it with a different key. He brought out stacks of bills that would take an eternity to count by hand, but thankfully they were rubber-banded and marked with amounts. I added them up in my head when he was done and sighed internally as I realized the total was incorrect.

"There you go," he said, pointing to the bundle.

"I was told to collect two hundred thousand," I said in as mild a voice as I could manage. "That's only one hundred thousand."

Short Guy's thick eyebrows rose. "Were you, now? Is that what your boss told you?"

"Yes."

Short Guy crossed his arms. "Well, maybe you should tell Maurice that his last shipment was short twenty ounces and if he wants to collect, he'd better send what he owes us."

He leaned forward and made a point to leer at me. "Unless you want to pay us back yourself, eh, *chica*?"

Dustin had been lying. This was a test.

I could take the money he offered and return, but Maurice would boot me out. The setback wasn't entirely the worst. After all, assuming that they didn't kill me, I could still weasel my way back into the bar for the staff meeting. However, if they did make an attempt on my life, my cover would be blown and we'd have done all of this undercover work for nothing.

Conversely, I could make a stand here to these three and try to get the money Maurice had sent me to collect. My odds were awful. I didn't have a gun, and based on their behavior, all three of them were demons. If I was going to play this hand, I'd have to do it perfectly. Zero room for error.

Leave. Fight. Negotiate. My only three options.

God, it was so great being me.

I let my gaze rove from demon to demon, analyzing them one by one. *Well, here goes nothing.*

"Gentlemen," I said calmly. "Why don't we end this debate like civilized individuals?"

"Oh?" Short Guy snorted. "How do you suggest we resolve this issue, *morena*?"

"By being truthful with each other," I said, unzipping my coveralls halfway. "I'll go first. My name isn't Jessica. It's Jordan."

I tugged the hem of my V-neck down over the upper part of my chest. "Jordan Amador."

Short Guy and Fat Guy didn't flinch, but Handsome Guy did a double take. He stepped closer, examining the scar, and his face went slack with shock.

"No shit," he said. "The Commander's Wife?"

I didn't quite wince. "Sure, if you feel the need to use my title."

"No way," Fat Guy said. "I heard she died the night she iced Belial."

"Does this scar look fake to you, tubby?"

He scowled at me. "If you're the genuine article, what the hell are you doing working for Maurice?"

"Long story," I said, letting the hem snap back up over my ruined skin. "The short version is that I want him and his gang out of the way. That means we have a common enemy. I think you three are smart enough to know what to do."

Handsome Guy nodded. "The enemy of my enemy is my friend."

"Exactly. So if you give me the money, I can continue with my plan to royally screw Maurice and his demons' nest over."

"And we're just supposed to believe you're gonna let us walk away alive?" Fat Guy said. "I've heard the stories, Seer. You're like a tiny African-American plague."

"Afro-Latina plague, thank you very much," I said, rolling my eyes.

Fat Guy set his glasses aside, shoved his chair back, and stood, towering over me. "Look, *puta*, why don't you take your ass back to wherever it belongs before I send you back in pieces?"

I cast a cool glance over him and then looked at the other two. "Am I to assume he speaks for both of you?"

Handsome Guy touched Fat Guy's shoulder and pulled him back. "Chill out, Ortega. Think this over. With Maurice gone, we can inherit the rest of the product lines in town. By the time he got topside again—if he even does—we'd be running the show. This is a business opportunity."

"We shouldn't deal with her kind, Alejandro," Ortega spat. "She works both sides. Once she's done screwing them over, she'll come for us."

"Not if you cut a deal with me right now. It expires as soon as I walk out that door."

"Oh yeah?" Short Guy said. "What if we just kill you?"

I shrugged. "Go ahead. But keep in mind that Gabriel knows I'm in town and it won't take him very long to retrace my steps. Would you like God's personal messenger knocking on your door and asking what happened to his little sister?"

Short Guy's expression didn't change, but I saw his Adam's apple bob up and down as he swallowed. Sure, I wasn't that intimidating, but every demon on the planet had seen Gabriel in action. He was sweet and wholesome as apple pie, until you crossed him. I'd seen him smite demons firsthand. It was awe-inspiring. Also, shit-spewingly *terrifying*.

"And that's assuming he gets to you first," I continued, a slow smile crawling over my lips. "What do you think will happen if Michael finds out?"

I'd gambled on that last threat. Some demons knew he and I had called it quits, but word hadn't quite spread through the entire supernatural community just yet. I crossed my arms so that they couldn't see that I wasn't wearing my wedding band.

"She's right, Manolo," Alejandro said. "I think it's worth the risk. Maurice has been shorting us for months. We were already talking about taking him out anyway. Let her do the job for us."

Manolo frowned. "And when she betrays us?"

Alejandro laughed. "We're demons, *pendejo*. We'll just add her to the list."

Ooh, there was a list. I was just racking up the popularity points with the demonic community. Lucky me.

"So," I said. "Do we have a deal?"

Manolo and Alejandro met eyes. The latter heaved a sigh and nodded. "Fine."

"Screw this," Ortega snarled. Then he grabbed me by the throat and slammed me into the wall behind us.

The office pinwheeled before my eyes. My skull and shoulder blades throbbed sharply with pain. Full-blown panic crept up through my chest like a scalding wave, but I shoved it down. My entire persona snapped back to what it had been before my undercover ruse: survival, above all.

I didn't give him the chance to crush my windpipe. I reached inside my bra, pulled out Gabriel's golden feather, and plunged it straight into Ortega's left eye.

The huge demon screamed bloody murder and dropped me, clutching his face. Acrid smoke and the stench of burnt flesh filled my nostrils as I staggered up to my feet, my eyes locked on the injured demon.

"You little bitch!" he roared, and charged me, his blackened eye clamped shut. He swung a meaty fist at my head. I ducked at the last second. His fist smashed into the wall above me and punched a hole through it. I swung up with the feather's tip and hit him dead in the groin.

Ortega screamed again and batted me away. I smacked the far wall, gasping for air as the impact had driven it out of me. I was still seeing double, but it looked like Manolo and Alejandro were letting us sort it out on our own; both of them were standing by the desk, as if waiting to see who would emerge the victor. Bastards.

"I'm gonna blow your goddamn head off!" Ortega bellowed, reaching for his gun...only to find it gone.

I drew my hand out from behind my back, brandished his .9mm, and smiled sweetly. "Made ya look."

I shot him in the head twice.

He collapsed back to the floor, dead as a doornail.

I watched his corpse twitch a few times and then used the wall to push myself all the way up until I was standing straight. I let all the emotion drain out of my features as I turned to face the remaining demons in the office.

"Anyone else want a go?"

After dropping the cash back off to the begrudgingly impressed Maurice, I instructed the driver to take me to a little ice cream parlor a few blocks from the Columbian restaurant and stepped onto the sidewalk as I spotted Myra sitting outside sipping a milkshake from beneath a hilariously enormous sunhat. Her version of undercover was at least slightly more subtle than mine—she wore a white sundress with a black belt across the middle, which drew attention to her impressive bustline, and had cat-eye sunglasses.

If the ghost sitting next to her had been visible to normal people, they would have looked like they were on a date, as he wore a tailored blue suit and burgundy tie. It was hard to explain how he was sitting on a chair considering he was incorporeal, but the gist of it was that ghosts could concentrate and be able to still obey the laws of physics somewhat. When a person died with unfinished business, it left them tied to the earth, almost like a weight around their ankles. However, they weren't completely whole, so all ghosts had no visible feet since they walked between the world of the living and the world of the dead.

I'd found Domingo about an hour after I met Jon at the park. He looked to be in his late thirties and he was soft-spoken and polite. I'd told him what I was and that I would help him find his inner peace so he could crossover into the afterlife, but that I needed his help with an important case before that time. He agreed to help and I'd sent him into the Kiln to spy on the demons and to tell Myra where they'd sent me without having to use my cell phone.

"Still alive, I see," Myra said, smiling lightly as I approached.

"Just barely," I said, ruefully rubbing my sore throat. Myra pushed her chocolate milkshake over to me and I partook of it liberally. The cold soothed the dull ache around my neck for now. I'd have to ask her to heal it later.

"Are you guys alright?" I asked.

Myra lowered the sunglasses enough to give me an incredulous look. "I'm having lunch with a dead guy. You do realize that?"

I rolled my eyes. "You think that's weird and not the fact that you have a raging hellbeast for a pet back at home?"

She shrugged. "It's all relative."

I took a seat and smiled at Domingo, who nodded to me. "How are you?"

"Still dead," Domingo said with a faint smile. "So that's not great, but otherwise, I'm fine. I'm glad you're okay. I wish I could have helped you when Ortega got nasty."

"Well, I walked out alive and that's all that matters. Can you give me a report of what you found out about the Kiln?"

"Yes, of course, but…" He nibbled his bottom lip, his brow furrowing. "I'm afraid you're not going to like it."

"Why not?"

He sighed. "The basement is indeed where they keep the cash and shuttle the product to the buyers, but…there are people down there."

My eyes widened. "You mean…workers?"

He nodded. "I stayed long enough to hear that they aren't other demons. They're prisoners. Slaves, basically. They count the money, package the heroin, and do other demeaning tasks that the demons force them to do."

I shut my eyes. "How many?"

"Fifteen."

"Shit," I said softly. "Goddamn those monsters."

Myra watched me carefully. "What do you think we should do?"

I steepled my fingers and pressed them to my lips, mulling the new facts over in my head. "How long did you watch over them?"

"All night. Once they're done working, they go into the cellar and sleep. I didn't see any way out other than the front door."

"Do you think the angels knew about the captives?" Myra asked me.

I shook my head. "They definitely would have made a move on the demons if they had. Still, I don't know if it's enough motivation to get them to mobilize a strike to save them."

Myra grimaced. "Look, I know what I said before, that I don't want the angels involved, but…"

She shook her head. "This is bigger than me. Than my boys. Call Jon and see if he'll meet with us. We can't let those people be slaves to the demons. We have to get them out, no matter what."

I nodded. "Alright. Let's go."

For obvious reasons, the places where demons met were called "nests" because it reminded one of a rat's nest or an equally undesirable creature that dwelled in a dark place. Angels, however, had a different term. The one I'd read in Andrew's journal was "haven" and that made perfect sense. Jon told me to meet him at an art museum, and it seemed rather haven-y to me.

Like most traditional art museums, the walls were high and strikingly white so that whatever painting or sculpture lay upon it would stand out more. It was late afternoon, so there were plenty of people in nice clothing strolling through the labyrinth of the museum, talking in soft tones and sipping the complimentary wine offered by the staff members. It turned out that Jon was an art dealer by day, which was by far the most interesting occupation I'd seen so far from the angels I'd met over the years. It made sense. I could listen to that accent for hours if you let me. He had a terribly soothing voice. Y'know, when he wasn't yelling at me for being reckless.

We didn't have time for me to dress up before going, so I felt extremely out of place in my jeans and boots as we walked in and asked the girl at the front counter for Jon. She looked rather skeptical when she saw me, but she called for him and he met us a minute later. He was dressed to the nines in a sharp black suit, no tie, the first button of his collar undone and his thick hair brushed away from his face. He did a bit of a double take when he saw the ghost next to us, but gestured for us to follow him.

He led us through the gallery to the large room at the end of the museum that was mostly empty. One of the staff members offered us wine. Myra partook. I didn't. Wasn't much of a wine connoisseur. Gabriel had tried to teach me the differences between types of wine, but it never stuck.

"Well," Jon said evenly, eying the three of us as we stood in a close semi-circle around him. "What was so urgent that you called for a meeting?"

I nodded towards Domingo. "Tell him what you told us."

He did. Jon downed his wine, handed the glass off to someone, and sighed deeply. "Father above. That certainly does change things."

I took a deep breath, dreading the answer, but I asked the question anyway. "But does it make it better or worse?"

"Unfortunately, that is not my call to make. We aren't like the demons here. Angels operate as a democracy. We have to agree on an issue before we make a choice to intervene. I will have to call a staff meeting and see if they will agree to a rescue mission."

"Are you shitting me?" Myra spat. "You have to have a committee to save a bunch of heroin slaves?"

He fixed her with a hard stare. "Myra, you must understand how things work down here. It's not the same as your human authorities. The angels tread a very thin line. We can intervene to save as many souls as possible, but we cannot risk inciting a war. Thousands will perish if we make the wrong choice. There are other ways to save them."

"How?" she demanded.

"If we tip off the police, there is a chance that we can save those people without the demons retaliating against the city."

I shook my head. "I think you know better. The cops move too slowly, and if Maurice has people that work for him there, they'll just clear them out and find somewhere else to set up shop."

"It's not my first choice. I agree with you that we should take them out, but I am just one person. We must get the angels to agree as one."

"How long with that take?"

Jon checked his watch. "The gallery closes at five. I will call a meeting afterward and we'll vote tonight."

"And if they say no?" Myra asked.

Jon exhaled through his nose. "We will have to find another way. Something more subtle than a siege."

"This is ridiculous," Myra snapped. "You're holding these people's lives in your hands and you have the power to save them, and yet you'll do nothing if a few stuffy angels say no."

"Myra, we have had this discussion before," he said sharply. "Our mission is the salvation of *all* mankind. Any goal that contradicts it is strictly forbidden. If you wish to take issue with someone, then perhaps you should consult with the Almighty."

She stepped in close, and with her heels on, they were the same height. Jon didn't back down. Neither did she.

"Call Him up," Myra whispered through clenched teeth. "I'll cuss him and his Son out. I don't give a shit about red tape. You told me that my job is to save people. I'm not going to sit on my ass and let those people die slowly under Maurice's boot no matter what your buddies say."

"Guys," I said, gently pushing them apart. "Don't slug it out until we've heard a verdict."

She scowled and turned away, marching over to one of the portraits to cool off. I gestured towards her and Domingo nodded, going over to help soothe her temper.

"Is..." I struggled with his name. "...Gabriel going to be there?"

Jon shook his head. "No, he's on mission elsewhere. I've been keeping him apprised, though."

I smiled weakly. "Tell him I said hi."

"I shall." He watched me for another moment. "You are not what I expected, you know."

"How so?"

"I've heard stories that you're cold and ruthless. Not what I see."

I crossed my arms beneath my chest. "Yeah? What do you see?"

"A battered warrior," he said, his voice soft. "Someone who has grown tired of fighting, but won't give up until the work is done. I see why the Commander fell in love with you. You lead only because there is no one else. I think you're not meant for this life, but you choose it anyway to make sure no one else has to suffer...aside from you."

I didn't have a reply to that at first. It scared me a little that he could see all of that from such a brief interaction. I licked my lips and glanced away at the painting in front of me—beautiful brush strokes depicting brown, orange, yellow and red leaves. "How long do you think I can keep it up?"

He shrugged. "As long as you must. In that regard, I see why some angels are so bothered by you."

"Why?"

He smiled. "You're just like them."

Myra and I grabbed supper next door at a diner and waited for the gallery to close, and that was an effort in itself. I wanted to sit the meeting out, but Myra argued against it. She thought I would be able to convince the angels to listen to reason, whereas I was pretty sure they wanted nothing to do with me right now. The Leviathan incident was too fresh on their minds. More than a thousand angels had given their lives that night to save the innocent people on the M.S. Midnatsol—a cruising ship that had been in the path of the Leviathan when it awoke. Angels were immortal and could be reborn in heaven, but death was death. That pain was beyond definition. No one deserved to die more than once, and yet angels died over and over for our sake. I didn't want to face them knowing what I did, but she wouldn't let me chicken out, so I stayed.

No one can say I'm not accommodating.

Jon opened the door for us after all the customers and clients had left the building for the evening. He did a quick scan of the area to ensure no demons would see us entering and then locked the door behind us. He walked us through the gallery to a room at the rear of the building. He opened the door. Myra and Domingo went through first. I hesitated, glancing at the back exit.

"Jordan," Jon said gently. "Please."

"Frickin' angels," I grumbled as guilt gnawed at my gut. "Why do you have to be so polite?"

I forced myself to walk through the door. I entered a long, narrow room with a polished oak table. There were ten chairs on either side as well as two at each end. There were thirteen angels sitting and drinking coffee provided by the expensive cappuccino maker on the table at the other end of the room. They glanced up with curious looks at Myra and Domingo. I fought to keep my face blank as I saw some of their eyes narrow when their gaze fell upon me.

"Thank you for coming," Jon said, shutting the door. "I apologize for the short notice, but this is an emergency that requires our attention."

He held out a hand towards Myra. "Most of you are aware, but allow me to officially introduce Mrs. Myra Bennett, a newly minted Seer. This is Mr. Domingo, a ghost who has been helping Mrs. Bennett with a..." He paused, choosing his words carefully. "...a self-imposed assignment."

Jon then cleared his throat and gestured towards me. "This is Ms. Jordan Amador, an experienced Seer. Mrs. Bennett requested Ms. Amador's assistance with this assignment."

Jon set his fingertips on the table and all pleasantness fled from his voice. "We have unfortunately experienced an egregious oversight with the demons' nest at the Kiln. We already knew about the drug trafficking and the prostitution, but Mrs. Bennett, Ms. Amador, and Mr. Domingo discovered that they have been keeping innocent people in the basement of the Kiln. Fifteen lost souls are trapped down there right now with no way out."

The angels' expression sobered immediately. "I would like to put it to a vote that we help them rescue those people."

Murmurs arose. Eventually, a brunette female angel spoke up. "Is there any conceivable way for us to intervene so that the demons don't know it was us?"

Jon sighed. "I am not sure. Even if we mask our energy, if a fight were to break out, they would certainly notice."

"What are the specs on the building?"

"One way in, one way out, hence why we've never tried to mount an assault."

"What about if we tried to go when they weren't there? What do you know about their security?"

Jon nodded to Domingo, who stepped forward. "From my overnight observations, the demons have watchmen that stay in the basement with the prisoners 24/7. They would have to be dealt with, but there is a security system in play. If anyone tries to enter the basement without the code, it'll trigger a mine buried in the center of the floor that would level the entire place. As I understand it, it's in case the police were able to infiltrate to find evidence."

"Would it be possible to get the code?"

"Maybe. I'm not entirely sure. I think it changes nightly. The only ones I've seen access the basement have been Maurice and his second-in-command Dustin. They always lock up before closing the bar."

More murmurs. A male angel spoke up next. "So if we hit them at night and saved those people, what are the chances they would know it was us?"

"If we can take the guards out without them seeing anything, it's possible. They might assume the human authorities or their rival competition got wind of it. However, that's still not the end of it. Even if we save those people, they will surely bring in more.

That is why I wanted to call for a vote. It can't be a half-measure. Either we do nothing or we destroy the entire nest. Once the demons are sent back to Hell, they will scatter and find somewhere else to go. Some might return for revenge, but most prefer self-preservation over retaliation."

The male angel frowned. "You're asking us to go to war, Jon. That's exactly what we've been trying to prevent this entire time. We put out fires. We don't raze the city to the ground."

"What's the point of putting out fires at all if you're just going to pick and choose who you let burn to death?" Myra asked in a low voice.

He grimaced. "No one's saying we do nothing, but we have to look at the big picture here."

Myra snorted. "Boy, I'm getting real damn tired of hearing that from you people. Are you not the sword-swinging badasses who sent Lucifer and his goons packing a few million years ago? Since when does it take a Senate hearing to decide if you should rescue people being held against their will by a bunch of bloodthirsty monsters?"

"She's right," another female angel said. "We've been tiptoeing around the demons for too long anyway. We should take action and stomp them out. We can send out a request for backup if the demons try to retaliate."

Some of the other angels nodded in agreement, but I saw a few shaking their heads. A hard-edged female voice spoke over the rabble.

"What does the Commander's wife think about the situation?"

The sarcasm coated over "the Commander's wife" was clear. I locked eyes with a green-eyed short-haired blonde towards the back of the table on the right side. *And so it begins.*

"This isn't my decision," I said with no heat, or any emotion at all, in my voice. "It's yours. I'm only here as support for whatever you choose."

The blonde snorted. "Well, that's new."

"What is?"

"You listening to your betters."

Scalding heat rolled up my body one inch at a time. She was trying to bait me. I breathed in and out evenly and told myself to let it slide. "First time for everything."

There, a joke. At least I made an attempt. She scowled, having expected an insult, maybe. "Just what was your role in all of this, Commander's Wife?"

My stomach turned uncomfortably, but I forced the words out anyway. "I infiltrated the nest and retrieved information for Myra on how to bring them down."

"So that's the second time you admit to being in cahoots with our mortal enemies. Did you get a lot of experience working with Belial or does betrayal come to you naturally?"

Jon glared at her. "We are not here to be the judge and jury for this woman's life, Bailey. Stop this antagonistic nonsense at once."

"Bite me, Jon," she snapped. "You're asking us to work with someone who has a history of stabbing us in the back for her own gain. She could be in on it, for all you know. She could be leading us right into a trap."

Myra stomped towards her. "Do you want to see a stabbing right now, you little — "

I caught her shoulder before she could make her way to the table. "Don't. Let her blow off some steam. Not getting laid for all eternity tends to eat at you."

Some of the other angels actually chuckled at that. Apparently, this female angel was a little unpopular among her peers. Bailey's eyes narrowed to slits. She stood up this time and stalked over until we were inches apart.

"Really? Is that why you're so calm and laidback, Commander's Wife? Any chance that the valuable information you extracted was received while you were on your knees?"

My hands balled into fists at my side. Every instinct in my body screamed at me to punch that little button nose of hers right out the back of her skull. "Insult me if it makes you feel better. Doesn't change the fact that you all have a choice to make. So make it and get the hell out of my face."

"Is it hard to face the truth, Seer? To look us in the eye knowing that you royally screwed us all over for the archdemon Belial? You may be brave and capable, but you are not one of us. You never will be. Stop pretending to be the hero. Crawl back under that rock you came from and don't ever show your face again, or I'll stomp you like the cockroach you are."

I smiled sharply at her. "Belial tried that. Look where it got him. And you aren't half the warrior he is, bitch."

She took a swing at me, but Jon grabbed her before the blow could land. "Enough! You're benched, Bailey. Outside. *Now*."

She struggled against him, reaching for me, her face red. He jerked her away from me and dragged her to the door, barking at her to stand down. By the time he reached the doorway, she'd realized he wasn't about to let her fight me and stomped out into the gallery alone. Jon shut the door behind her and straightened his ruffled jacket.

The angels were all staring at me now, their expressions unreadable yet unnerving. It was too quiet in here.

God, I wanted to go home.

"Look," I said finally. "No one in here has to march in this parade with me. I know what I've done. I'm certainly not proud of it, and I don't expect you to understand, but it's not about me. It's about fifteen innocent people who haven't seen the light of day for possibly years. Forget me. Think about them. Think about the other people we can save if we shut down their organization. We'd be killing two birds with one stone. No more demons, no more drugs. You guys are back to just stomping out regular old sociopaths, killers, druggies, and whatnot. And if you don't trust me, then I will sit in this room from now until the raid is over so that you know I haven't betrayed you."

I took a deep breath. "Please. Please help them."

Silence pervaded the room. Jon glanced around at the many faces and cleared his throat.

"All in favor of assisting the people held captive at the Kiln, say aye."

"Aye."

Ten voices.

"Majority rules," Jon said, a faintly relieved smile on his lips. "Let's get to work on a plan to save them."

CHAPTER SEVEN

"So I get the feeling that you don't have a sense of self-preservation."

I snorted into my Heineken bottle. "You're just now getting that feeling?"

Myra shrugged. "Hey, I'm not always perfect at reading people."

"You were the one who scraped me off the floor of that warehouse," I said, lowering the sweating green bottle to the top of the bar. "I would have assumed you knew that about me."

A sobering thought entered my mind. "I take it you were there when they grabbed me?"

"Yeah," she said softly. "There were too many of them that day and I didn't have my rifle or I'd have stopped them before they…"

She licked her lips, leaving the sentence to dangle there painfully. No more words needed, really. I wouldn't have blamed her anyway. She saved my life. End of story. The details didn't truly matter in the end.

"Lost track of you for a bit," she said a while later. "The mutt picked up your scent and eventually we found you."

"Remind me to thank him."

Myra smirked. "He won't care."

"Sure, but it's the principle of the thing."

We drank for a while. It was one of those nights where I was allowed to break my dry streak. We were one day away from breaking into a demons' nest. It could be my last day alive. Still, I didn't want to spend the precious cash for some good whiskey, so

I settled for a beer instead. I could remotely stand Heineken, at least.

The bar we'd chosen was one of Myra's favorites. It was just your average sports bar, but she knew the bartender from her days as a bouncer and he gave her half off anything she wanted. Various games — football, baseball, hockey, basketball, soccer — droned on in the background, punctuated by masculine howls of either praise or damnation when someone made a big play. I didn't mind the noise. It was...comforting, in a way, to know the world spun on even when it felt like mine was about to end.

"You should have punched that bitch," Myra grunted.

"She could have kicked my ass if I did."

"Still. She deserved it, accusing you of being the demon's whore."

I sighed. "Doesn't matter. I don't give a shit about my reputation at this point."

"Liar," she said softly, glancing at me. "I saw the way you reacted. Even if you're guilty about the breakup, you took the insult personally."

"So what if I did?"

"Look, I remember what Gabriel taught me when I became a Seer. Letting something like that fester inside you is a bad idea. Are you sure there isn't anything you want to get off your chest in case tomorrow is our last day on this rock?"

I shook my head. "It doesn't matter. None of it matters. So what if I come back as a ghost? It's better than where I'd be headed."

"Bullshit," she snapped. "Are you telling me you believe that bitch now? You think you're bad news? Is that why you came all the way to Houston to save my kid and my husband? Is that why you risked your life getting information when no one else would?"

"She's right about me," I mumbled. "I'm not a hero. I do this because I have nothing else left. I don't have a family. I don't know what the hell I am anymore."

"No one does, Jordan. No one on this blue marble has any idea what the hell they're doing and that's why we bond with each other, human or angel. We all screw up."

I glared at her. "Have you ever screwed up so bad that over a thousand people died because of you?"

"No. But I have seen people die because I didn't stop it. Numbers don't matter. Intentions don't matter. You're still trying to save people and that's what counts, not your motivations."

She drained her bottle and motioned for the bartender to get her another one. She popped the cap off and took another swig.

"You know what's crazy?" I murmured.

"What?"

I almost smiled. "If I wanted to, I could call Belial right now and tell him to shut down this whole operation and he'd do it in a heartbeat."

Myra stared at me, her piercing eyes half-lidded. "No bullshit?"

"No bullshit."

"Wow. What's it like having an archdemon as your booty call?"

I let out a hollow laugh. "You know, maybe that's what kills me the most. I probably wouldn't be this screwed up if I actually had given in to him. It's like you have a vault full of drug money and the key is just sitting in your pocket every day and you have to wake up and come up with a reason not to use it. I hate knowing that I could have everything I want if I just said yes to him. Sure, I'd forfeit my soul, but it hasn't been doing me that much good to begin with at this rate. I'm just...drifting."

"Maybe you are," she agreed. "But that's not what makes you who you are. Maybe you look at yourself and just see the scars, but it isn't a reflection of you as a whole. Sometimes the only way to do the right thing is to just keep saying no to that tempting offer."

I pressed the cold bottle to my forehead. "I know. But how long until he breaks me? He told me I'm the only one who has ever held out this long. He's been alive for millennia. What if he's right?"

The question hung in the air like suffocating humid mist. After a while, Myra grinned and slapped my shoulder hard.

"Don't be stupid. Men are never right, babe. Come on. It's time to go."

She dropped me off at my hotel. I did my usual ritual of peeling off my makeup and collapsed in my bed. I wanted nothing more than to sleep, but I knew that there was a good chance You-Know-Who would be waiting for me. I'd been too tired to do it before, but tonight was important. Possibly my last night to sleep. I wanted to be left the hell alone, literally.

I rolled onto my back. I still couldn't access my energy without blowing my cover, but I could construct mental shields without exposing myself as a Seer to the outside world. Belial had taught me. It was like building a brick wall. I held that image in my mind and constructed the wall one brick at a time until I felt satisfied that he couldn't break through it. Then I rolled over and went to sleep.

I dreamt of my mother's kitchen.

Catalina Amador was the most beautiful woman I'd ever seen, but I supposed all little girls thought that about their mothers. She had long, wavy black hair, beautifully arched eyebrows, one of those lovely aquiline noses, stunning cheekbones, and full lips. Like me, her skin was a rich brown. I could always just barely hear her accent as a warm undercurrent when she spoke English.

Right now, she stood at the small counter across from the little round dinner table she and I ate at every night, chopping the bright red and yellow bell peppers that would go into her homemade paella. There was a little girl with a frizzy ponytail seated at the table with a spelling workbook spread open. It was me, age five, doing my homework.

Every so often, my mother would smile at me and gently correct me, or tell me that I'd done a great job on something. The little five-year-old me preened each time she got a compliment and swung her tiny bare feet back and forth as she started the alphabet song again, this time in Spanish. My mother had always stressed that our heritage wouldn't determine where we ended up in life, only our intelligence and perseverance. She knew that teaching me her native tongue as well as English could someday give me an advantage. She wanted me to be prepared, to have a chance out there in the world.

I stood at the entrance to the kitchen, trembling in disbelief that I could see my mother in front of me for the first time since my brush with death a couple of years ago. I almost never could remember her clearly, and any time that I did, it was a nightmare of when I'd been taken away from her to live with my abusive Aunt Carmen.

I stepped forward to talk to her, to touch her, to hug her, to tell her that I loved her more than anything, but I ran into some kind of invisible force-field. I flattened my hand against it and something pushed against my fingers. I realized with a start that it was my mental shield. How was it keeping me out? Had I just bottled it all up over the years to protect myself from the pain? This hadn't ever happened before. I didn't even know I was capable of such a thing.

Unless it wasn't me at all who had done it.

"You know," a quiet male voice spoke from behind me. "I never had the pleasure of meeting her, but I heard she left quite an impression."

I pressed my forehead against the invisible wall. "Get out."

"You know full well that you don't truly want me to go."

I whirled on Belial. "This is *my* memory. This is my life. You have no place here. Now get out or so help me God, I'll kill you with my bare hands."

"Even though I can help you?"

"Stop it!" I screamed. "Just stop it already! Stop lying, stop manipulating, stop following me around and just let me rot in peace!"

He stared at me with those icy eyes. "No."

I tried to punch him, but my center of balance was off because I was shaking so hard with rage and grief and desperation. He leaned to one side so that my shot missed, but I launched myself at him, clawing and scratching like a wild animal. He just wrapped his long arms around me. I struggled to get free, but it didn't really matter. I was broken. Completely, utterly broken.

"Why?" I whispered. "Why can't you just leave me alone?"

"Because you don't deserve to be alone, Jordan."

"You don't know what I deserve. We're both monsters."

"Perhaps we are." He tilted his mouth towards my ear. "But we don't have to be lonely monsters."

"Why did you show me this?"

"Because the past is poison," he said softly. "Indulge in it too often and you'll lose your life. There is nothing left for you back there, Jordan. Memories at best are warnings. Precautions. Aesop's fables with a lesson to be learned at the end. Take what you can from them and let them lie or you'll fade into dust alongside them."

"I miss her."

"I know. She is with you nonetheless."

I slowed my breathing and let his words sink in finally. He was right. I was scared and unsure of myself. Memories were easy to lean upon in hard times. I could lose myself in the way things were and not have to face what lay in front of me.

I untangled myself from him. He let me, but he kept my hand in his as I faced the invisible wall. I rested my hand on it and watched the sunlight spill through the window, giving the little kitchen its own holy glow. I smiled through my tears and shut my eyes. When I opened them again, it had disappeared. Instead, I stood in the bedroom of my old apartment. It had hardwood floors that creaked and groaned, the bathroom was laughably tiny, and it was always too cold, but I loved it.

"I might die tomorrow," I said absently, staring out the window that used to face an apartment complex on the other side of the street.

"You might," Belial agreed.

"Is this the part where you lecture me about being reckless?"

"No. This is the part where I make you a better offer."

I wiped my cheeks clean and faced him, tugging my hand free. "Then this is the part where I tell you to shove it up your lily-white ass."

He inhaled deeply, as if trying to be patient with me. "Considering the alternative, perhaps you should hear me out."

"Why? What has changed since the last time, Belial? I know what you want. I may not have much to live for, but it's still my life. I won't be your puppet for all eternity."

"Oh, Jordan," he said softly. "How wrong you are. You've known me all this time, and yet you still don't fully understand what I'm offering."

"Really? And what's that?"

"Freedom."

"From what?"

"Yourself."

I froze. "What are you talking about?"

"You are a very particular kind of woman, Jordan," he said, and then started to circle me one step at a time. "Prideful. Stubborn. Cynical. Altruistic. Self-sacrificing. Diligent. Powerful."

He went around three times and then stopped directly behind me. "Alone. In spite of all that you've done to save the human race, here we are. You remain unhappy and solitary because fate doesn't care about what is fair. You have had everything taken away from you one by one until only you remain."

I swallowed hard as his words sunk into my skin like thick, gelatinous poison. "So what? That's life."

"No, that's not life. All this time you have assumed this is the lot that you have been dealt, that it is your responsibility to carry these burdens until your knees buckle. You've been blinded by the promise of heaven, by the lie that when all is said and done, you will waltz into the Father's arms and bask in the land of milk and honey. You've been fed a lie, Jordan. It's nothing more than cheap manipulation by the Almighty to get you to play His game, to be His servant when you could be something more..."

He leaned in towards my ear, letting the last two words drop into it like a secret. "A goddess."

I shut my eyes. "I won't join you just for an ego boost. I know what you want. I'm not turning my sword on the angels."

Belial sighed. "Why do you see the world in black and white? The world is shades of grey. It's not good versus evil. Everything comes down to choice, and they've led you to believe that you don't have one when you do."

"What choice?"

"The choice to be truly free of both sides."

"That's not possible."

"Oh, but it is. Do you think I cannot provide that for you? That I cannot find you a place where nothing can touch you, neither man nor angel nor demon? No one said you had to live this wretched calling forever, Jordan. This is not about what I want. This is about what you deserve."

I gasped as his fingers slipped beneath the hem of my dress shirt and his fingertips lightly grazed the scars on my back. No two were alike; some were thick, the ones that had torn open my skin so badly they had to rush me to hospital for stitches, others thin and crooked as a garden snake, all of them too deeply inflicted to ever heal. "These scars that you wear like armor are preventing you from seeing the truth. You have let them define who you are. These painful, damning memories have convinced you that you are nothing but a tool to be used to deliver their falsehoods of justice. You use them to remind you of the monsters that lurk in the darkness."

He slid his hand higher up my back, sending soothing shivers wherever his fingers touched my skin. "I can lift that burden, sweet Jordan. I can free you from these shackles you've unknowingly entangled yourself in. I'm not asking you to raise arms against the Father, against the angels, against mankind. I'm simply asking you if you think that your soul is worth more than what they have offered for it."

He trailed his hand around towards my side and pulled me back against him, his lips brushing my ear, his words soft and sweet, yet dripping with filthy promises. "I know exactly how many nerve endings there are in your body. You could spend days, weeks, months, even years in endless ecstasy. I can do things to you that no man on this earth has even dared to discover. You could finally rest and be at true peace, without any preoccupation, free to do as you please without repercussions or penalties or fear of damnation."

Belial swept my hair to one side and kissed my neck, traveling down towards my shoulder. "I would be at your beck and call, only there if you dare ask it of me, never when you wouldn't want me. You could be free, Jordan. Never be forced to make another decision you didn't want to. No more ultimatums. No more deals. No more sacrifices."

He lifted my hand to his mouth and kissed my palm. "No more nights spent alone. Just you, me, a bed, and the darkness as our companions. Can you look me in the eyes and tell me that isn't something you want?"

I closed my eyes. He wasn't wrong, damn him. "I…m-my husband…"

"He walked out on you," the demon whispered. "Tell me, Jordan. Have you heard one word from him since it happened? Has he made even the slightest attempt to ensure that you are alive and well?"

Something inside my chest withered. "No."

"Don't let him hold you back from what you want. As you said before, this is your life. The choices you make from now on are yours and yours alone."

I didn't realize he'd been unbuttoning my dress shirt until the material slipped off my shoulders. He cast the shirt aside and ran his hands over my hips, my waist, holding me in place as he lowered his mouth to my shoulder blades. He kissed the sensitive space between them and then trailed his mouth down to where my scars began. I shivered as those soft lips traced them carefully, as if trying to commit them to memory. It had been so long since I'd been touched, held, pampered, spoiled with attention. Pleasure simmered up through my skin. I'd missed it.

Belial climbed higher until we were level again and slipped my ear lobe into his mouth, sucking gently, and all thought of resisting him left me. I could have this. No one would know about it. Just me and him. No more pain. No more terrible responsibilities.

I shuddered as he licked my neck, his hands unbuckling the large button to my jeans. He slid one hand inside them and a wave of sweet, sweet ecstasy washed over me. I leaned my head back onto his shoulder helplessly.

And saw myself in the mirror of my vanity.

I barely recognized the woman staring back at me through mussed dark hair and dilated pupils. I looked nothing like myself.

And it scared the hell out of me.

I shook my head. "No."

"Hmm?" Belial said distractedly, his mouth at my neck. "What was that, my pet?"

I slid away from his intoxicating, maddening touch and shook my head harder. "No. I...can't do this. I won't do this."

"Why?" he demanded. "Why, damn you? You have nothing left to lose, you've said so yourself."

"It doesn't matter what I want," I said, wrapping my arms around my bare stomach. "If I don't do this, people will die."

Belial caught my face between his hands. "People die every minute of every day, Jordan. What difference does it make?"

"I know they do. But these are ones that I can save."

He searched my gaze for a long moment and then rested his forehead against mine. "You are by far the most aggravatingly stubborn woman I have ever laid eyes on."

He kissed me before I could say anything in return. "And I cannot wait until the day when you realize that the person who needs saving is you."

I woke up the next morning alone.

Dammit.

I showered. Savored the scalding water sliding down my back. Lathered with leisure. Washed my hair with the cheap hotel shampoo and conditioner. Focused on the simple act of cleansing my weary body one inch after another. *One step at a time, Amador. You can do this.*

I blow-dried my hair and flat-ironed it, tucking it up into a high ponytail. Took my time globbing on makeup. Boy, I wouldn't miss this part of my cover.

I packed my stuff up and opened the door.

To find a cop waiting for me.

The same cop I'd seen while driving Maurice's van.

Well, shit.

He was dark-haired and probably in his early-to-mid thirties. The cop who had been driving the car was a patrolman, but this guy looked to be a detective of some sort based on the clothing: black blazer, white-dress shirt, slacks, and dress shoes. His shield was clipped to his belt, shiny and intimidating under the morning sunlight.

To be fair, at least he wasn't standing directly outside my door menacingly. He was leaning against the metal banister across from the room smoking a cigarette. He glanced up at me with brown eyes and said, "Good morning," without an ounce of malice.

"Morning," I said carefully as I shut the door. "Weird spot for a detective to hang out. Although, that's certainly none of my business."

"Usually, no, but I think you and I should have a little chat. My name is Hughes."

"How can I help you?"

"We met briefly yesterday while you were driving that van."

"Is there something wrong with that?"

"Afraid so," he said, taking another pull. "Considering whose van it was."

He was fishing for something. I'd seen cops do that before. The good ones were experts at manipulation, waiting for the suspect to trip up and blab on themselves. The best method was to just keep my mouth shut and move it unless he had a warrant or a reason to arrest me. However, I'd have to gamble to find out if he actually had anything on me.

"Look, unless you work for an employment agency, I have nothing to say to you. Have a good day, Hughes."

I started to walk away, but he spoke up. "The last three people we've arrested that drove that truck went to prison for five plus years a-piece. The four before that ended up dead. Maybe I don't work for an employment agency, but I know what happens to the people who work in that bar. We know they're connected to the drug runners at the Columbian joint. We're closing in on them. Is that where you want to be?"

I took a deep breath. "You assume that I have a choice."

"You always have a choice, Mrs. O'Brien."

I flinched. Couldn't help it. He kept going. "Yeah, I know who you are. I watch the news every night before bed. Saw that fiasco in Lexington. You have quite a reputation, Mrs. O'Brien."

"Amador," I said sharply. "It's Amador. And if you had any sense, you'd realize maybe that's my motivation right there. I was a wanted criminal. Not exactly a lot of jobs I can get after that, not even with a pardon from the Big Guy in the Oval Office."

"Don't bet on another coming your way if you continue associating with the people in that bar. I'm only going to make you an offer once. Cooperate. Help us take them down and you'll be immune to what's coming."

I shook my head and muttered, "Doesn't matter what side I'm on; someone always has a problem with me."

"What was that?"

I turned. "I appreciate what you're trying to do. You may not know it, but we're on the same side."

He eyed me. "We are, huh?"

"There's no way I can convince you right now, but if you haul me in, good people are going to suffer for it."

"Is that a threat?"

"No. Just a fact. Give me today. Just today. Then I'll be out of your hair and you can continue keeping the city safe."

Hughes pushed off from the banister and narrowed his eyes at me. "Is there something I need to know about, Ms. Amador? Withholding crucial evidence that could lead to a conviction is just as big a crime as aiding those bastards."

I gritted my teeth. "I don't have time for twenty questions. Either arrest me or back off."

We stared each other down for a while. He finished his cig and extinguished it on the banister, tossing it into the garbage can nearby. A thoughtful smoker. How nice.

"Enjoy your day, Ms. Amador," Hughes said in a quiet but utterly firm voice. "I'll see you again soon."

He turned the corner and disappeared. Sadly, I knew what that was code for too: he was going to tail me for the rest of the day. Great. Like I didn't have enough shit to deal with.

I waited until I was safely inside a cab before calling Myra. "Things just got infinitely more complicated."

"How's that even possible?" she asked, sounding as tired as I looked.

"I picked up a pigtail."

Myra groaned loudly in my ear. "Are you fucking kidding me?"

"I wish. He grilled me outside of my hotel room just now."

"Is he one of Maurice's men? Do you think your cover's been blown?"

"No, he doesn't read like a demon. I saw him when I went to deliver the shipment to the Columbian place. I think someone's actually been trying to take them down on their side, but they don't have the evidence to make a move. I'm new in town, so maybe he wanted to get the jump on me and see if I'd roll on Maurice."

"Fantastic. That means he's following you. So where are you gonna go?"

"I'm going to try to give him the slip at the mall. If I manage to pull that off, I'll call you when I'm on the way so we can finish up the You-Know-What."

"Good luck. If the guy's with vice, they are pretty damn good at tailing people. Don't underestimate him. Be careful, and don't be surprised if he's got a partner."

"I'll do my best. Bye." I sighed, hung up, and then told the cab driver the address.

And today began with such promise.

For the record, there wasn't really a manual to teach you how to ditch a tail. My life operated in the shadows and I knew how to ditch a demon — mainly because it involved cornering them and murdering the shit out of them — but I hadn't ever needed to get rid of a nosy cop before. Sure, I'd watched a bunch of movies in my time, but that didn't mean I knew how to do it. I'd have to go the *Batman Begins* route: theatricality and deception. Who says movies don't teach you anything?

There were a lot of malls in the city of Houston, Texas. I'd just picked the one I'd seen on the way into town: the Galleria Mall on Westheimer Road. It was enormous and gave me plenty of opportunities to possibly lose the cop. I wanted to do it quickly, in case Maurice was having me followed too. If they saw me anywhere near a policeman, the plan tonight was finished and we'd have no chance at rescuing their hostages.

The cab dropped me off. I walked inside in search of a good place to switch out my clothing. Hughes would have mentally memorized what I'd been wearing and so changing my outfit would give me an advantage. Plus, at least I could get rid of the dirty money Maurice had given me. I'd hated accepting it, but now I could put it to good use.

I stopped in the Ralph Lauren store and bought a nice burgundy floral-patterned dress, leggings, ankle boots, a hat, and sunglasses. I bound my hair in a bun and tucked it beneath the hat and threw some jewelry on for good measure. It cost a pretty penny for the get up, but I looked nothing like myself. They gave me a bag to put my old clothes in and then I left the store. Naturally, like any good detective, I didn't see him anywhere outside of the store, but my gut told me he hadn't lost me yet, so I headed further into the labyrinth of the mall.

I headed towards the central atrium of the mall and turned down one of the longer halls and got on the escalator. I glanced behind me, trying to be as subtle about it as possible, as I rode above the level of the crowd. He wasn't on the escalator behind me or in the main part of the hallway. Just as I reached the top, I spotted a glimpse of him at the corner where I'd turned into this part of the mall. He hadn't walked around it yet, but I could see his reflection in the window of the storefront across from where he stood. I had a good bit of a lead on him, unless he knew something I didn't, which was entirely possible. Myra had mentioned a partner. I'd have to be on the lookout.

I went to the nearest bathroom after I reached the second level, waited a solid ten minutes, and then poked my head out. There were a couple of parents waiting for their little ones in the hallway, but no one else so far. I checked to see who was within view of the bathroom hallway across and to the side of the entrance. No Hughes. However, I saw a skinny black-haired teenager who was pretending to use his phone glance right at me quickly and then move aside.

Alarm bells rang in my head. Cops didn't use teens, not when they were scoping out a criminal. What the hell was that kid's story?

I left the bathroom hallway and did another sweep of what I could see as I headed towards one of the department stores. Still no Hughes. Either he'd blended in really well or I'd gotten the drop on him. Something told me it wouldn't be that easy.

I ducked into the ladies fitting room of the Macy's and waited yet again. Once the busy period cleared up and there weren't any women left inside, I inched my way over towards the exit and listened in. Sure enough, I heard two male voices.

"You want to tell me what you're doing following her?" Hughes said, his voice edged with annoyance.

"Oh, of course. None of your fucking business."

"The badge makes it my business, kid. Kick rocks."

"Boy, you guys are something special, aren't ya? I never did figure out why the Master didn't tell us to just wipe you all out. Maybe we lost the first war, but I doubt we'd lose a second one."

I paled. Oh no. Please don't let that mean what I think it means.

"Look, either you make tracks or I'll let you sit in holding downtown for the rest of the day. Your choice."

I heard the teenager snicker. "Try me."

"Your funeral."

Hughes was a pain-in-the-ass, but I wasn't about to let some punk demon shank him. I stepped out of the fitting room right in front of Hughes, narrowing my eyes at the teenager.

"Can I help you with something, kiddo?"

He was disturbingly thin and disturbingly tall, probably around 6'4", with yellowed teeth from chain-smoking and short, jet-black hair that had been heavily oiled. He wore a Punisher t-shirt and baggy cargo pants, which let him blend in perfectly with the demographic he'd been going for. Demons often wore this disguise because it made normal people pay them no mind. No one would expect a seventeen-year-old to split a man in half.

He grinned at me, one hand in his pocket, probably palming the blade he'd been thinking about stabbing Hughes with. "Don't know what you're talking about, lady. I'm just waiting on my girlfriend."

"Lucky girl," I said. "Let me guess. Manolo and Alejandro want you to report in on my progress?"

"Never heard of 'em."

"Great. Then stop following me or you can join your buddy Ortega downstairs in the sauna."

The grin faded slightly. I'd struck a nerve. He at least had an idea of who I was since the threat to send him back to Hell seemed to land.

"Lotta talk for such a little girl," the demon said, and his voice came out so many octaves deeper that I heard Hughes stiffen behind me in surprise. He'd dropped the act, somewhat. "Feeling cocky since you got the Boy in Blue as your backup?"

"Not especially," I said. "I'm trying to ditch him and you're screwing it up for me."

"Really," he said, the disbelief clear. "So what if I tell Maurice you're in bed with the cops? What do you think will happen?"

I kept my face blank. "Go ahead. But I'm pretty sure that's counterproductive for your operation."

He shrugged. "Maybe, maybe not. Either way, you should watch that tongue of yours. It'd make a great addition to my collection."

Hughes put a hand on my arm and moved me aside. "Did you seriously just threaten her in front of me?"

The demon sent him a bored look. "Settle down, junior. The grownups are talking."

Hughes glared. "Hands behind your back. Now."

"Oh, happy day," the demon said. "Finally, some action."

"Stop!" I barked, shoving one hand against Hughes' chest as he surged forward. "I don't have time for this shit. You want a piece? Take it outside. If we cause an incident, all three of us get our covers blown."

The demon growled. "The hell do I care?"

"You can't report back if you're dead or arrested for assaulting a cop and a civilian. Now either meet me outside to settle this or piss off."

He glanced between me and Hughes for a moment. His hand was still in his pocket. If he went for it, I could probably get to Hughes' gun after he went down and put one between the demon's eyes before mall security arrived. My palms got clammy with sweat. Adrenaline made me hyper-attentive to every breath coming out of his nose, searching for a reason to eliminate him.

Finally, the demon snorted. "Not worth it. For now, anyway."

He lumbered off towards the door, but then stopped, smiled, and pointed a finger-gun at Hughes. "Be seeing you, detective."

He walked into the mall and out of sight. I exhaled and dropped my hand from Hughes' chest finally.

"Goddamn, girl," he growled when I faced him. "How deep are you in this shit?"

I offered him a weary smile. "You don't wanna know. Nice work, by the way. I didn't know he was following me until I had to start looking for you."

"You're welcome," he said with the utmost sarcasm. "Now will you listen to common sense?"

"I would if I had a choice, trust me. By the way, I'm sorry."

He eyed me. "Sorry for what?"

"The headache you're about to have."

I punched him in the temple as hard as I could. He slumped to one side, unconscious. I caught him before he hit the floor, dragged him into the nearest fitting room stall, and closed the door. It wouldn't take long for someone to find him, but I didn't have a choice. I had lost too much time already.

Man, was he going to be pissed off when he woke up.

I took the back exit out of the Macy's and hurried around to the nearest curb, called a cab, and drove off by the time I heard sirens in the distance.

CHAPTER EIGHT

I didn't take the cab straight to Myra's place. Once Hughes woke up, he'd get a team to call all the cab services and cross-reference them with eyewitness accounts until he figured out who picked me up from the mall, and then ask the cabbie where he took me. My gut said Hughes was good and scary when he was angry, so the cabbie would give me up in a heartbeat. Instead, I took the cab to a bus station not far from Myra's neighborhood and then hoofed it all the way there, trying to keep a low profile. Mass transit meant that if Hughes did track me there, the people who would've seen me would be elsewhere by the time he came a-calling. With any luck, this whole nasty debacle would wrap up tonight and I'd be out of Houston for good. I had no desire to cross paths with him again.

As for the snotty teen demon, there was no sign of him after I left the mall. I checked my surroundings as thoroughly as possible and didn't see hide nor hair of him. Maybe the warning had worked, or he finally learned to keep his distance like a professional. The latter seemed more likely. He'd probably reported back to Manolo or Alejandro and they berated him into staying out of my way until the dust cleared.

I used the spare key to open the door to Myra's house and nearly tripped over Ace, who had been lying on the rug in the foyer like a good watchdog. He snarled at me. I snarled back. The hellhound rolled his burning red eyes and settled down again, his crimson gaze fixated on the door.

I was about to call out to her, but I heard her voice coming from the kitchen. She was on the phone and the conversation was definitely not going well.

"Look, we don't need to be having this talk right now, Charlie," Myra said, her back to me as she smoked and stared out into the backyard. "You're supposed to be on vacation."

A pause. "Yes, I know it was spur-of-the-moment. No, I'm not in any danger. No more than usual, anyway. Jordan's on the up-and-up. I can vouch for her. Since when do you not trust me, huh? I thought that was in the fine print for this whole 'marriage' thing."

Another pause. "Yes, she's got a past. So what? I've got one too. Is that a deal-breaker for you all of a sudden?"

Guilt made a sour taste in my mouth. From the sound of it, she hadn't told him about what we were up to and he knew that her orders to take their son Chris out of town meant she was in trouble. I'd seen what this kind of thing could do to a healthy marriage firsthand. They certainly had their work cut out for them. I couldn't imagine having to worry about a child in the middle of all this death and destruction. Then again, yes, I could. I'd done a lot to keep little Juliana safe and to get her back to her mother. I'd only felt a tiny sliver of that overwhelming fear of protecting someone's baby girl. Words failed to describe how terrible it was to feel helpless to stop something from happening to an innocent kid.

I cleared my throat loudly. Myra craned her neck at me and sighed out a mouthful of smoke.

"We'll finish this later. I gotta go. Give Chris a kiss for me. Bye."

She hung up, brushed some stray hair behind one ear, and gave me her usual confident smile. "So you gave the cop the slip, eh?"

"Are you sure you want to go through with this?" I asked quietly.

The smile faded. "Are you serious?"

I nodded once. "Dead serious."

"What? Did your eavesdropping make you think I'm having second thoughts?"

"No," I said, setting my bag aside. "I'm the one having them. You have a lovely family, Myra. You have a home. You could lose all of that tonight. I just want to be sure that you've considered all your options. Revenge looks pretty on paper, but the truth is that even though you get that thrill once you've carried it out, the consequences overshadow that feeling. When the bill comes due, it won't be pretty."

I licked my lips and measured my words. "It happened to me. I'd like it if I could prevent it from happening to you."

Myra watched me for a while through the faint haze of smoke surrounding her. She put the cigarette butt out on an ashtray. "I appreciate your concern. I'm not the type to tuck tail and run, especially when the stakes are this high."

"I'm not asking you to run. You could just…abstain."

"I could. But if things go south and someone innocent dies because I decided to abstain, then I might as well have pulled the trigger myself. We done?"

I resisted the urge to sigh. She was stubborn to a fault. Maybe we had that in common. "Yeah. I'll catch you up on the way. Let's go."

Myra grabbed her stuff and whistled for Ace. The three of us piled into her truck and got on the road to perdition.

We drove to the art museum, parked around back, and made our way to the conference room with the bomb in tow. One would think that made for a very tense drive over, but I'd lived this lifestyle too long to even think twice about it.

Jon and the other angels were already inside prepping equipment and passing out copies of the floor plan. He looked a bit relieved as we walked in. Domingo waved from where he stood beside them. We set our stuff down—carefully—and he got us caught up on their progress.

"Everything set?" I asked.

"Yes," Jon said. "We have everything we need."

"So what's the final say on the plan?"

"You will attend the staff meeting tonight. You'll go into the office, disable the guards in the basement, and disable or contain the bomb. After we have confirmation, we'll storm the building and exterminate the nest. Once everything is clear, we'll extract you and the prisoners and get you all to safety."

Jon gestured to Domingo. "He has agreed to help keep watch to warn you of danger and to act as a distraction to the guards once you open the basement door. He'll also contact us once you've disabled the mine so you don't have to risk wearing a wire."

"Great. Well, if you're going to have fun storming the castle—" Myra smirked and shook her head at me. "—what about the cops? They're naturally going to hear the ruckus."

"We've staged a riot on the other side of town to keep them busy. We'll also have many of the streets leading in blocked off with fake construction signs to stall long enough to get everyone out. Then we'll level the place with the bomb you provided to get rid of any remaining evidence."

"What about me?" Myra asked. "Maurice told me to be at this meeting if I didn't want to end up worm food. Won't he send someone to my place to see where I am?"

"We'll have someone waiting for them."

"And that won't tip them off at all?"

"It shouldn't. The angels will only intervene if they try to do something dramatic, like set the place ablaze. Maurice will simply think you declined his offer and headed out of town. He'll be dead long before he has time to retaliate. I sent my best angels off with your husband and son this morning. They will be safe. I promise."

Myra's shoulders relaxed the tiniest bit. "So then where am I in this equation?"

"Your sharpshooter skills are what we'll need most of all," Jon said, sliding a map of the block surrounding the Kiln over to her. "We'll have you on the rooftop across from the parking lot. Shoot any demon who tries to run."

Myra grinned. "With pleasure."

"What about the mutt?" She jabbed a finger in the direction of the hellhound, who had curled up under the table not long after we arrived.

"Since we can't vouch for his loyalty—"

An indignant, resounding "*Rrrrr*" floated up from underneath the table.

"—he will stay with you. After the building has been destroyed, he will make sure nothing emerges from the wreckage. Hellhounds have an excellent sense of smell and can tell if someone's faking."

"Last thing," I said. "What about the leftovers at the Columbian joint? Won't they just pick up where Maurice's operation left off?"

"We're going to let them believe that," Jon said, smiling fiercely. "But we have something special in mind soon after."

"A man after my own heart." I rolled up my sleeves.

"Alright. So which one of you is going to teach me how to defuse a bomb?"

When you go to war, you want to be prepared. You gear up. You clean your guns and hone your fighting skills. You bring your A-game and prepare to stare the enemy in the eye before you pull the trigger.

And apparently, if you're me, you bring barbeque.

Dustin had been annoying me all day long by sending me dick pics, but I had to admit the look of bewilderment on his face as I walked into the bar with a huge, deep container of ribs was pretty damn funny.

"What the hell is that?" he asked, locking the door behind me as I walked in.

"What?" I said. "You told me it was a meeting. Man's gotta eat, right?"

"Yeah," he chuckled, pointing me in the direction of the kitchen to my right. "Just didn't see that coming. You're awful sweet for a career criminal, Jess."

"Why, thank you."

The kitchen was tiny, naturally, since the place didn't serve anything more than beer nuts and the occasional basket of fries. I set the ribs on the counter facing the doorway. Dustin took a peek inside, groaned, and stole a rib, admitting that he hadn't eaten anything in a few hours. One thing to love about Texas was that there was no shortage of good BBQ places. Fine place to go for a last meal, honestly.

"You're still surprising me after all this time," Dustin said with a sigh after he'd eaten and wiped his mouth clean with a nearby paper towel. "Though I have to say I'm a little hurt that I didn't get a response to any of my...messages."

Oh, he'd gotten a response, alright. Myra had to talk me out of bleaching my eyeballs earlier. I channeled my inner strumpet and forced myself to press up against him, dropping my voice to something I hoped was sultry. "I got them. I'm glad you have an appetite. Tonight's going to be...special."

He wrapped his arms around me and gave me a squeeze. "Glad to hear it. Been looking forward to this, gorgeous. Trust me, you won't regret it."

It wasn't hard to smile. "I suspect I won't."

I gave him a quick kiss and sent him off, telling him I'd get the ribs on plates for the other guests. He left me to be domestic, and as soon as he was gone, I lifted the rib container to reveal what I'd been actually trying to smuggle in: the bomb. Homemade bombs were a thing of beauty. Some were small enough to even fit inside a large purse, but since I hadn't ever carried one so large any time I came into this bar, I needed something more inconspicuous. Not long ago, I'd happened upon a brick of C4 while on a case and kept it since I knew it could be handy later on. Once it had been outfitted with a remote detonator, it was good to go.

I actually did put the ribs on plates and bring them out to the other demons, who gave a mixed reaction of amusement and bemusement. However, after they were all distracted with the food, I tucked the bomb beneath my bomber jacket—cue rimshot—and snuck into the women's bathroom. I made sure it was empty, locked the door, and then got out the screwdriver I'd stuffed into my boot to get to work on Phase 1 of the plan.

Maurice's office stayed locked at pretty much all hours and I had no hope of stealing the key. The blueprints had revealed that the air ducts connected all three of the rooms on this side of the building, meaning I could gain access that way without anyone seeing me. All I would need to do is pay attention to most of the meeting, excuse myself to use the bathroom, and then go after the basement. Domingo had been here for hours, hiding in the walls and spying until he'd seen today's combination for the basement entrance. He'd slip down there before me and distract the guards while I took them out and then went for the mine.

After I took out two screws, I lifted the dusty grate away from the wall and tucked the bomb in the corner of the duct for safekeeping. I shut it, screwed it back in place, and then went back out into the bar.

The gathering had brought forty-eight demons into the Kiln. Once upon a time, I'd have been so scared that my knees would knock together, but I knew that playing the part was the difference between life and death. I swept through the room and pretended as if I were the life of the party, confident and lovely, hanging on Dustin's arm and laughing at all his terrible jokes. After everyone ate, Maurice hushed the crowd and took a seat at the bar alone, while everyone else sat facing it.

Forty-five minutes slid by. Maurice droned on about the heroin and its buyers as well as the prostitution ring they were currently getting set up on the west side. I leaned in and whispered to Dustin that I had to use the ladies room and slid out from under his arm.

Once the bathroom door was locked, I launched into action, unscrewing the grate and crawling inside. It was a good thing I was slender — the fit was tight enough to make John McClane claustrophobic. I had to scoot the bomb in front of me with one arm and squeeze myself along the duct until I reached the one that led to the office. I wriggled until I could reach the screwdriver and undid the screws to the grate. Once I'd eased it down, I took nearly a full minute and let my eyes adjust to the darkness. No lights, since that would tip someone off that I was in here. Quietly, I sifted through the drawers of Maurice's desk until I found the flashlight Domingo had mentioned earlier and then walked over to the floor safe.

Domingo phased through the wall a moment later, looking rather nervous for a dead guy. Couldn't blame him. Even if he was physically unaffected by what would go down tonight, it was a lot of stress to put on a troubled soul.

"Are you alright?" he whispered as I dusted off my shoulders and hands.

I nodded. "Ready?"

"Yes. The combination tonight is 48-72-35. There is a ladder that goes down about twenty feet. The guards are both standing near the entrance. They have walkie-talkies that will alert Maurice's bodyguard. You must attack as quickly and quietly as possible so they can't tip him off. The prisoners have done their work for the day, so they are in the sleeping area to your immediate left. I will go down first. Wait about ten seconds and then follow me."

I nodded again. "If something goes wrong, tell the others to move in with or without me. Got it?"

He frowned. "Jordan—"

"My life's not important," I said, narrowing my eyes at him. "You have to warn the others if something happens to me. You're the only one who can."

Domingo sighed. "Very well. Go ahead."

I put the combination in carefully. I heard a soft click to confirm that I'd unlocked it. Domingo slipped down through the floor and vanished from sight. I began to count.

Ten.

Nine.

Eight.

Seven.

Six.

Five.

Four.

Three.

Two.

One.

I reached for the latch to open the basement door.

"Surprise, surprise."

I froze.

Dustin flipped the light to the office on.

"Guess I don't know you as well as I thought, gorgeous."

CHAPTER NINE

I didn't move a muscle. Not even to turn my head to see Dustin standing beside the door. My peripheral was enough, and so was the deathly calm tone of his voice. How in God's name had he gotten in here without me seeing or hearing him? I'd vastly underestimated him, second banana or not. I was in very deep shit.

"You know, I've pictured you on your knees about a thousand times," Dustin said casually, locking the office door. "Just not this way."

I heard a sharp metal click. He'd undone the safety on his Glock. Shit.

"Put the bomb on the desk. Slowly. If you even breathe wrong, I'll put a bullet between those beautiful brown eyes of yours."

Shaking, I rose inch by inch and placed the block of C4 on Maurice's desk.

"Turn around."

I swallowed hard and angled myself towards him.

Dustin had the kind of face built for smiling. He had lines near his eyes, creases near his mouth, and with that sunny grin, he could promise you the moon and you'd believe him. Now I saw an emptiness in his expression that was the exact reason my heart vibrated in my chest at the speed of light. Demons were hollow. They were predators. They were built to tell us sweet lies and then devour us when we least expected it. He may have been charming and amiable, but now I'd peeled off the human mask to reveal the monster beneath.

"Y'know what the worst part is?" Dustin asked quietly.

I forced my hoarse voice to respond. "What?"

He let out a dry laugh. "I actually genuinely liked you. I mean, I've been doing this shit for a long time. Screwed all kinds of girls and tossed them aside when I was done. Not one of 'em turned my head…'cept you. I wasn't even going to turn you into a prostitute after I was done, you know. Most of the women we attract in this business just want a fix or want someone to pay their bills or just plain want attention. I finally find one that's different, and she works for the fucking Son of God. Figures. Maybe this is how Uriel felt after Zora betrayed him. Poor bastard."

I licked my lips. "How did you figure it out?"

"The barbeque ruse was brilliant. I actually didn't put it together until I went back for seconds. I could smell the residue from the C4 in the bottom of the pan. Checked the bathroom. You weren't there. And I'm awful quiet when I want to be."

"That's a first."

He chuckled. "Gun pointed at you and you're still a smartass. Goddamn if I don't love that in a woman."

He stepped towards me. "Hands up higher."

Fear spread through me in a cold, agonizing wave. This was it. Final curtain call.

I waited for him to tear my throat out, but he didn't. Instead, he reached for my collar and tugged my shirt down over my chest until the scar was exposed.

"Shit-goddamn-cocksucker!" he hissed and then let go. "The Commander's Wife. I cannot believe I was this stupid."

"To be fair," I said with a weak smile. "I'm apparently super good at faking demons out."

"Guess you are. I'm going to pat you down. Don't get cute."

He held the gun to my chin and peeled the bomber jacket off my shoulders. He tossed it on the desk and then performed a relatively thorough pat-down with just his free hand. I knew I'd hurt his feelings because not once did he feel me up. Great.

In the movies, if I were the heroine of the story, I'd snatch the gun away and then turn it on him, but this was real life. It wasn't how much pressure it took to pull the trigger — it was the reaction time. Dustin was a supernatural creature hiding inside a meat suit. He could react a thousand times faster than I could, so I'd be dead as soon as the command to snatch the gun went from my brain to my sluggish human hands. The only way to possibly get out of this alive was to get him distracted.

"So what's the plan then?" he asked tiredly once he was done. "Plant the bomb and blow us all sky-high? Who hired you to do it? Did the angels not want to get their hands dirty?"

"If you know who I am, then you know I'm not going to talk."

"I'm trying to be nice," Dustin said. "If you tell me now, then I'll soften the blow when I tell Maurice. I'll say you cooperated and he might go easy on you."

"Bullshit."

His blue eyes hardened. "Do you really want to know what he's going to do to you without me vouching for you? I have worked for him three centuries now. You can't imagine the shit I've seen him do. I know exactly what he'll have planned for you, Commander's Wife."

Aha. A bright spot of hope opened up inside me then. He was taking it personal. Good.

I hardened my voice. "I'm shaking in my boots here, demon."

"You should be," he whispered, lowering the gun. He wrapped his hand around my throat and tilted my head, his lips pressed to my ear, his stubble scraping my cheek. "He won't kill you. He won't even torture you. He's going to send you to a spa for five straight days. They'll exfoliate your pores, give you a deep tissue massage, a top dollar mani-pedi, and then a makeover that would make Hollywood starlets jealous."

His voice dropped to subzero temperatures. "Then he's going to bring you back here, strap you into a stockade naked, and then rent you out by the hour."

I started trembling again. "That's right. Ten thousand dollars an hour to fuck the archangel Michael's wife. And he won't care if the demons are nice about it. No matter what they break, he'll fix it. He'll leave you in some deep, dark hole for the rest of your youth until you either agree to do it willingly or you go mad and try to kill yourself. You won't see the light of day ever again and no one is going to save you because no one will know where you are. Then maybe if you survive it all, he'll chop you into little pieces, decorate a cake with them, and then mail it to Michael on his birthday."

Dustin reared back until we were face to face again. "However, if you tell me what you and the angels are planning, I will put in a good word for you. Instead of that fate, I'll just keep you as a pet instead. Sure, I'll take my frustration out on you for a while, but after that it'll be easy street. Maybe one day I'll get bored and give your boyfriend Belial a call to come collect you and you can go where you belong."

"You would do that?" I whispered. "You would stop Maurice from turning me into a whore?"

"I was telling the truth before. I do like you."

"What if…" I bit my bottom lip. He glanced at it. "What if I sweeten the deal? Will you go easier on me in the long run?"

"How sweet are we talking?"

"Maurice won't come looking for you just yet. We have maybe ten, fifteen minutes. I could…*apologize* for betraying you in that amount of time. I'm really good at apologizing. Ask Belial."

Dustin chuckled darkly. "Goddamn, that's a silver tongue. No wonder I fell for it the first time I heard you in this bar. Now you wouldn't be trying to trick me with the offer of sex, would you, Commander's Wife?"

"Me? Never."

He smiled. "Pants on fire, gorgeous."

"What choice do I have? It's not like I can strong-arm the gun away from you. This is the only card I've got left to play. I'm choosing the lesser of two evils here."

He tapped the barrel of the gun against my hip, staring down at me as he mulled the thought over. Finally, he shrugged.

"One quickie couldn't hurt."

He didn't take his hand off my throat as I lowered myself onto the desk, flat on my back. He kept a firm grip on the gun and used the barrel to nudge the hem of my shirt over my navel. Lust filled his eyes at the tiny sliver of smooth brown skin. I reached and pulled it to just underneath my bra and he groaned low in his throat at my flat, tight stomach. He lowered his mouth and kissed my navel, tracing its shape with his tongue. He moved higher towards my chest, and realized he couldn't keep both hands full if he wanted to get anywhere, so he let go of my neck and motioned with the gun.

"Shirt. Now."

I took it off. His breathing doubled in speed. He licked his lips. "Girl, you are just all kinds of pretty."

I smiled. "I taste even better."

"I bet you do." He leaned over my chest, tracing the shape of the scar with his tongue. I shivered.

And I watched until the barrel of the gun was no longer pointed at my head.

I made some convincing heavy breathing noises and carefully slid my hand into my discarded bomber jacket that he'd tossed on the desk earlier. My fingers closed around the handle of the screwdriver.

Dustin moved up towards my neck, the gun all but forgotten in his hand as he left stinging kiss marks over my breasts. I wrapped my legs around his waist, drawing a pleased grunt from him, and waited until his first finger loosened around the trigger of the gun.

Then I plunged the screwdriver straight through his throat.

Dustin choked.

Hot blood splashed down onto my bare skin, so hot it nearly burned. He froze, his blue eyes bulging in total shock, his heavy body convulsing above me. I knocked the gun away and clapped my other hand over his nose and mouth so that he couldn't scream. Red bubbles gurgled out from either side of the wound in his neck. Weak, slurping, disgusting noises escaped as he kept trying to breathe. I pinned him against me and held on tight as his body began to spasm on top of me.

"I want you to remember this moment for the rest of your immortal life, Dustin," I murmured. "Don't fuck with a woman on a mission."

He was staring straight into my eyes when he died.

Carefully, I maneuvered out from under his heavy corpse and made sure it stayed on the desk. My bloody hands shook with tremors as I pulled my shirt and bomber jacket back on and hurried over to the basement entrance, blindly hoping we could still salvage our plan. I clutched the blood-soaked screwdriver between my teeth and held onto Dustin's gun. The office was sound-proofed, and so was the basement. By now, Domingo would've reported to the angels outside. I was on my own, at least for the time being. I had to move fast or everything would be in vain.

I heaved the heavy door to the basement open and was greeted with darkness. The office light provided a spotlight down to a concrete floor. Luckily, one of the guards wasn't standing directly under it. I spit out the screwdriver and cleared my throat.

"Who's there?" a male voice called up from the darkness.

"Hey, I need your help. Gimme a hand here, will ya?" I asked, putting as much authority into my voice as possible. If I sounded like I belonged there, they might buy the ruse.

Twin pairs of footsteps approached. I kept the gun behind my back until they were close enough to peer up at me through the hole. With the light spilling in from the office, they couldn't see my face, but I wasn't about to give them enough time to anyway.

I whipped out Dustin's Glock and shot them both in the head. They slumped back onto the concrete floor and I quickly slipped down into the basement, pulling the latch behind me and locking it.

I didn't waste a second double-checking my accuracy. I put a second bullet in each of their skulls and made sure they didn't have pulses before examining the basement.

As the blueprints had described, the room was long, ice-cold, and the concrete walls were bare. Straight ahead of me were plain wooden tables that had bill counters perched on the corners. The adjacent wall had black file cabinets lining it end to end, probably full of confidential files and contacts. The basement was dimly lit with fluorescents, giving it an eerie atmosphere even more than knowing what went down in this awful hellhole. The far wall had several waist-high safes that I assumed was where they kept the bulk of the cash. Each one had an electronic counter on the outside detailing how much was inside. I tallied it up to $2.5 million altogether. Crime really did pay.

So did payback.

After walking through the room once to be sure there weren't any other guests hiding in its depths, I tucked the gun in the back of my jeans and headed towards the thick, black velvet curtain that hid the living quarters of the captives.

My heart shuddered.

Obviously, they'd heard the gunshots. Fifteen bodies were all smushed against the farthest wall, clutching each other and trembling with fear. Their sleeping area was nothing more than rugs piled all along the floor. There were two toilets on either corner, and a showerhead in a tiny alcove nearby with a drain in the floor. The area didn't have good lighting, so all I could see were fifteen pairs of wide eyes glinting at me like frightened raccoons.

I walked towards them slowly, my voice hushed and as soothing as I could make it. "Hey there. Don't be afraid. I won't hurt you. My name is Jordan Amador. You might have heard the demons talk about me. I'm a Seer. I work for the angels. I'm here to rescue you, okay?"

None of them said anything. Shit. Their faces were rather dirty, making it hard to identify any ethnicities. It was hard to tell if some of them were foreigners, or if they'd been mistreated so badly that they were afraid to speak. I couldn't imagine what the demons had done to them. My hands curled into fists. Every one of these bastards would burn for this and I couldn't wait to make it happen.

I took a deep breath and calmed my nerves. "My friends are coming to get you out. It won't be long. I'm going to make sure that no one detonates the bomb, okay? I'll keep you safe. I promise. Stay right here, alright?"

I pulled the curtain back to hide them, hoping it might make them feel even the tiniest bit safer, and walked into the center of the room. I shoved the tables aside until I had enough room to work. The bomb sat underneath a plain circular metal shielding, hence the need for my screwdriver. I unzipped the inner pocket of my bomber jacket and withdrew the homemade EMP device the angels had put together for me. It was about the size of a calculator and therefore didn't make an obvious lump in the jacket. It turned out it had been easier to teach me how to use it than to teach me to defuse a bomb in just one day.

I counted the minutes under my breath as I carefully unscrewed the metal shielding and calculated that I had less than five before Maurice would come looking for Dustin and me. Sweat beaded on my forehead and ran down into my eyes. My palms got sweaty. I tried not to think about Dustin's threat, but it hovered in my ears. *You'll die a slave, Jordan. You were a fool to come here.*

"Shut up," I hissed. "The cavalry is on its way. I'm not going to die in this shithole."

You should have taken Belial's offer. The angels will betray you.

"No, they won't. They'll come through. They always do."

Not for you. Not anymore. You're a dead woman walking.

Gritting my teeth, I lifted the metal shielding the barest millimeter up and peered beneath it, making sure there weren't any wires connected that would detonate the bomb if I uncovered it. None. I exhaled and put it aside before aiming the homemade EMP device and letting off a blast. The few working lights inside the bomb blacked out. There. It was done.

Just as it did, the entire building rattled.

I jumped to my feet on instinct and peered up at the ceiling. Bits of concrete fell out and hit the floor. A stupidly optimistic grin stretched my lips. The angels had made their grand entrance.

Which meant that the shit had hit the fan.

Quickly, I started stacking tables on their sides across from the basement entrance as makeshift cover. I did the same for the living quarters of the captives and counted how many rounds were left in the Glock. Fifteen. Better not miss if someone came to play.

I knelt behind the stacked tables and shut my eyes, channeling the cool, distant monster inside me that could shoot without hesitation and without fear.

Several nerve-wracking minutes passed. I cursed the demons' foresight to make this place soundproof and waited anxiously, hoping that Domingo would phase back through the wall and tell me everything had gone perfectly and I'd be walking through a sea of corpses to deliver these innocent people to the help they needed. I prayed for it to happen. I'd damn well will it into existence if I had to.

Unfortunately, Domingo didn't appear.

I heard the unmistakable metallic wrench of someone opening the basement door. I lifted up over the table barrier and aimed. No light shone down. Whoever had entered the office turned off the lights. Great.

"Jordan…Amador…"

My blood ran cold.

"Five-foot-six, one-hundred-and-twenty-four pounds, scar on the left breast, along with others on the small of the back, size six shoes, brown eyes, black hair, speaks Castilian and Mexican Spanish, no siblings, deceased mother, unknown father, lives in a one bedroom apartment in Albany, New York, and got married to the archangel Michael in a courthouse surrounded by friends and family."

A dry chuckle trickled down around me. "I remember reading that file over a year ago. I always knew it would bite me in the ass that it didn't have a picture with it."

I heard no movement. I saw no movement. But that didn't mean jack-shit. Maurice knew who I was now and he was positively gleeful about it.

"I can see why you got Belial so twisted up that he can't see which way is up any more, lil bird. You're quite the actress. I look forward to teaching you some new tricks for my clients."

"Show me your face," I said. "I'll teach you one right now."

"You have the bollocks of a person ten times your size, Ms. Amador. Just because I intend not to kill you doesn't mean you should be mouthin' off to me. I can still piece you back together if I tear a few things off ya. After all, you did kill my best friend."

I snorted. "Demons don't have best friends. Dustin was your lackey, and you're lucky I killed him the nice way. You don't want to know what I had in mind before he ambushed me."

"Let me guess: you're going to bomb us all, eh? Makes sense. Nice and clean. While I respect your tenacity, I have no plans with the undertaker today. Be a good lil bird and drop the gun. If you do that, I'll go easy on you. If you don't, I will get *nasty*."

That last word echoed around me like a thousand ravenous wolves baying into the night sky. I had no idea how he managed to create that effect with his voice, but it sent chills frosting through every inch of my body. It felt as if he'd said it straight into my ear. Fear gripped my lungs and made it harder to breathe, but I wasn't about to let him scare me.

I slapped on a sharp-toothed smile. "Well, you know what Janet Jackson says. Nasty boys don't mean a thing, demon. Let's see what you've got."

"Very well, Ms. Amador."

The tables in front of me exploded.

I fought down a scream and threw my forearms up, shouting, "In the name of the Father, I reject!"

At long last, my spiritual energy burst free from inside me. Cool, bright, uplifting energy coursed through my veins and formed an invisible shield in front of me as the wood splintered into millions of deadly shards. They flew through the air in almost every direction, punching holes into the file cabinets and denting the safes behind me. Several lights in the ceiling popped out, leaving a dim glow in the center.

I landed in a crouch below the single remaining light, my eyes darting around in an attempt to figure out where the demon had gone. I couldn't hear anything; just my own shallow breaths and the blood pounding through my ears as I strained to listen. *Think, Amador. Think like a demon. Think like...*

I whirled around and opened fire. The sparks from the gun briefly illuminated the whites of Maurice's eyes as he swung his enormous fist at me. He lurched his head to one side so that the shot missed, but it gave me just enough time to dart out of the way. He punched a crater into the concrete floor, and just as quickly as he appeared, he vanished into the darkness again.

I dropped to one knee and slid the screwdriver out of my jeans, using the sharp edge to slice into my forearm. It only hurt for a second. I let the blood drip down across my palm and fingers and pressed a handprint into the concrete below me, listening the whole while.

"You know, I wouldn't have expected a woman with your reputation to risk her life this way," Maurice said casually, his voice projecting again as if he were in every part of this basement. "What motivated you? Revenge? Were you angry that I tore a hole in your little Seer friend? It wasn't personal. I needed her to cooperate. That's the one thing you humans never seem to understand. Compassion makes you a target. It makes you susceptible to manipulation. If you had any sense, you'd be a coldhearted murderer."

"Show me that handsome face again, Maurice," I whispered. "You'll see I've got that part down pat."

He chuckled again. "Not as much as you think, Seer."

He appeared in front of me. I whipped the barrel of the gun at him, and froze.

One of the captives was clutched in his fist.

It was a young woman with dark hair and brown skin. Her eyes were huge and filled with tears. Maurice had her pinned against the front of his body and he stared at me with those empty pits for eyes, a smile on his lips.

"See," he said. "This is why you should become heartless, lil bird. You know the name of the game. Drop the gun or I'll kill her."

"Fuck you," I murmured back. "Let her go."

"Your trigger finger isn't faster than my whole hand. We both know you're bluffing. I can crush her throat before the bullet leaves the barrel. Hell, I can move her head in the way before it gets halfway here. Drop the gun."

"Why? So you can kill her and every single one of them while I stand here defenseless?"

Maurice bared his teeth. "Smart lady. You've done this dance before, haven't you?"

"Yeah. I'll take my chances. Besides, we both know how this ends. You're stalling. You're hoping you can take me hostage and use me to bargain for your escape."

I laughed. "Well, joke's on you, Maurice. The angels don't like me. They'll shoot anyway. So would you rather die now or later? Your choice. Because I'm not dropping this gun no matter what you say."

His vicious smile faded. I watched the realization spill through him. He knew I was right. He knew this was the final curtain for him and his organization.

Which was why he shoved the girl on top of me.

I hit the floor, crying out as her body weight took me to the ground. In seconds, Maurice batted her aside and pinned my gun hand to the floor, his other one reaching for my throat. Time slowed down to nothingness. I saw the mad, unstoppable rage in his eyes. He was going to snap my neck.

I slapped him as hard as I could with my bloody hand and shouted, "With blood, I bind you to this spot! Walk no more until the spell is broken!"

Maurice howled in pain as the bloody handprint on his head ignited a fiery red and then the matching one on the floor did the same. His entire body convulsed as the blood magic ensnared him in that one spot, immobile, frozen. I threw myself to one side as he struggled to reach for me, but the blood spell finished taking hold and he crumpled in half, holding himself up by his hands and knees as crimson light pulsed around him.

His shoulders bulged so hard that they split the seams of his suit jacket. His eyes nearly popped out of his skull as he tried to fight the hold over him to no avail.

"Kill you!" he screamed. "I'll kill you, human! I'll rip you apart and feast on your soul!"

I offered my hand to the fallen girl and lifted her up, wiping the tears from her eyes. "Are you alright?"

She stared at me, open-mouthed. "W-Who are you?"

I smiled at her. "Nobody special. Let's get you out of here."

CHAPTER TEN

Have you ever watched a building explode before? It's pretty damn cool.

Then again, knowing that Maurice and his remaining scumbags were still inside while it blew probably made it more enjoyable for me. Better still, Myra was the one who detonated the bomb. Once the main explosions were over, she even went down and lit a cigarette off one of the flaming demon corpses. That woman didn't give a shit. She was a walking Honey Badger. Hmm…maybe there was something to that, actually…

Ace got to live up to his namesake after the blast. A handful of demons survived only to be torn into chunky salsa by the hellhound in mere seconds. He chased every last one down and shredded them with extreme prejudice. I was happy to be on the rooftop of a building far away. I didn't like thinking about the fact that I'd spent the night in the same house as him.

The angels loaded up the captives and took them to the nearest safe house to find out their names and where they'd come from. I stayed and watched the Kiln burn until there was nothing left but ashes. What a beautiful sight. Harry Dresden would be proud.

Afterward, Myra drove me back to her place just so we'd have extra security in case any of the demons in town hadn't been at the staff meeting. Jon promised his angels would watch over us carefully that night, and for once, I believed him. They hadn't said as much, but judging by the looks on their faces as I led the procession of innocent people out of the Kiln, their faith had been restored in me, even if it was just for one night.

I slept like a baby.

No dreams. No nightmares. Just quiet, peaceful slumber. I had missed that.

I woke up the next morning to murmurs coming from the foyer. Curious, I crept to the landing of the stairs and listened in. A male voice. Soft, caring, endlessly polite.

I brought both hands up to my mouth.

Gabriel.

"I am so very glad to hear that your impromptu mission was a success," my surrogate brother said, and I could hear the smile in his words.

"If it helps, Jordan tried to talk me out of it," Myra replied, and I could tell she was smiling too. "Might've had a point, but a man's gotta do what a man's gotta do."

"Apparently. While I did advise against such an action, I am glad you will be able to sleep safely in this city."

"Are you sure about that? What about the demons at the Columbian joint?"

"What demons?" he said, feigning innocence. "My dear, didn't you hear? There was an awful riot last night and their place burned to the ground. I heard there were only three casualties, though. How fortunate."

Myra laughed. "Well, that's good to hear. Everything's tied up in a nice little bow, isn't it?"

"For now." A pause, then Gabriel sighed. "My dear Mrs. Bennett, I again extend my deepest apologies. I have taken it as a personal failure that my people weren't able to protect you from Maurice."

"Look, maybe I wasn't as…receptive as I could have been to what you had to say. You warned me that trying to remain neutral was not an option. We are at war. You were right. Therefore—and I don't say this often—you're off the hook. And it may or may not be because you are one of the most handsome men I've ever laid eyes on."

Gabriel coughed. I smiled, because I knew from experience that she'd made him blush. "Why thank you, my dear. Even so, you have my word that your family, immediate and extended, is under our protection from now until the hereafter. We will not fail you again."

"Thank you, Gabriel. That means a lot to me."

"And…if you would be so kind…please give my love to Jordan."

The simple affection in his voice made tears burn in my eyes. He was only a few feet away from me. I could just race down these stairs and throw myself at him. I wanted to hug him. I wanted to smell his ridiculously expensive cologne and ask him where he bought the inevitably five thousand dollar suit he was wearing and take him to coffee and tell him about everything that had happened in the last few months.

But I couldn't.

That was my burden. It had been my mistake with the Leviathan and with Belial that cost me this friendship. If I went to him now, he'd be punished for it by the Father. Orders were orders. He couldn't see me until it had been ordained and we had been forgiven.

"She's right upstairs," I heard Myra say rather softly. "Tell her yourself."

He sighed. "There are some orders even I cannot disobey. But...if she were listening right now...I would want to tell her that I love her more than anything and I hope that she knows how very proud I am of what she has done for you and for the people of this city. I would want her to know that I hope to be reunited with her soon, and once she is in my sights again, I have no intention of letting her go. I would want her to know that I miss her smile and her laugh and her sarcasm every day, and that it won't be long before I take her to dinner and spoil her in spite of how much she hates it. I would want her to know that she is still my heart, even though we are apart right now. Will you be kind enough to tell her that for me, Myra?"

"Yeah, Gabe. I will."

"Thank you. You can reach me at this number if you ever need anything. Take care, my dear."

I heard the front door close. I collapsed to my knees, my shoulders shaking, sobs wracking my upper body, the tears overflowing because I'd been trying so hard to hold them in. I heard the stairs creak as Myra ascended them. She knelt beside me and rubbed my shoulder, smiling.

"Come on, you big baby. Let's get you some coffee."

My burner phone rang while I was putting my clothes back into my suitcase. I frowned, not recognizing the local number. After mentally flipping a coin, I answered.

"Hello?"

"Quite a mess you've left me, Ms. Amador."

Flat, hard, borderline humorless male voice. Oh, wow. "My sincerest apologies, Detective Hughes. But I did make good on my promise, didn't I?"

"I suppose you did. Though I find it hard to believe you alone are responsible for an entire bar exploding."

"You'd be surprised."

"Is that a confession?"

I filled my voice with an overdramatic tone. "You'll never take me alive, coppah!"

Hughes made a noise that wasn't quite a laugh. "Just so you know, I don't appreciate being left in the ladies room of a department store unconscious. When I got back to the precinct, there were twenty-seven copies of that shitty Zack Snyder movie *Sucker Punch* on my desk."

I coughed, trying to hide a laugh. "Oh. Yeah, that's unfortunate."

"Never been knocked out by a girl before. Pat yourself on the back."

"It wasn't personal. I swear. I was trying to do the right thing."

"I don't know if 'the right thing' can be defined as blowing up a bar full of drug-runners," he said, sarcasm coating practically every word. "But it's better than having to sit around and watch kids O.D. on the streets while your superiors keep telling you

~ 196 ~

'slow and steady wins the race.' I sure as hell ain't about to thank you."

He paused. "In lieu of that, you get a 24-hour pass out of Houston. If you're gone by morning, I won't come looking for you. Deal?"

"Deal. Thank you, detective."

"Don't mention it." He hung up. I tucked my phone in my pocket, smiling a little as I finished putting my stuff away.

A while later, my things were packed up in the back of Myra's truck. Ace jumped into the bed, walked around in a circle, and curled up on top of my large suitcase. I arched an eyebrow at him. "Seriously, dude? It's going to take me six months to get the fur off of that."

The hellhound stared blankly at me and then laid his head on his massive paws. I rolled my eyes. "Whatever, fleabag."

"It's a sign of affection," Myra said. "He's marking you. You're under his protection now."

I scowled. "Is that a real thing or did you just make that up?"

"Nope. Totally real. He did it to Chris' backpack and to my gym bag."

"Nothing of Charlie's, though?"

"Nope."

I laughed. "Oh. Well, that's…nice. I think."

"So what's next for you?"

"I got a tip from Jon that there's a new Seer in Dallas who needs some training. Figured since I'm already in his neck of the woods, I could stop by and give him some pointers."

"Want some company?"

I blinked at her. "Are you sure? I mean, we just wrapped up a big case. Don't you want to be here when the boys get back?"

"Yeah, about that…" She glanced away, staring into her neat little yard and up at her cute little house. "I thought about what you said. Maybe this isn't the way to keep my boys safe. Where I go, trouble ain't far behind. You heard Gabriel. He promised their safety and I don't want to throw a wrench in that."

"What are you proposing?"

She glanced back at me, grinning. "Wedding vows already? Fast ass."

I rolled my eyes. "Myra."

"Maybe me and the mutt tag along for the time being, until we figure shit out. You could use someone to watch your back and so could I. That way if Belial ever does come try to take a piece, it'll be his ass."

I bit my bottom lip. "Are you sure? I'm not easy to be around."

She arched an eyebrow. "Do I look like a basket of flowers to you?"

"I might get you killed."

"Not if I get you killed first."

"Gee, that's reassuring." I sighed. "Well, nobody lives forever."

Myra beamed at me, her brown eyes fierce and excited in the sunlight as she opened the door to the truck.

"Damned straight."

Oh, boy.

What the hell was I thinking?

FIN

Acknowledgments

To my mother and father, Bryan, Sharon, Aunt Nette and Darryl, and my extended family, I could not express my gratitude if I had another 200 pages to properly thank you for your support.

To Marginean Anca, your art is exceptional and I couldn't love this cover more if I tried.

To Andi Marlowe, thank you so much for your editing skills.

To my friends, thank you for putting up with me and for helping me survive writing this book.

To my readers, thank you for your amazing love and support. You are the reason this book exists.

To my fellow authors and colleagues, thank you for your energy and encouragement and the opportunity to be among you.

CPSIA information can be obtained
at www.ICGtesting.com
Printed in the USA
LVHW081309091019
633680LV00014B/518/P